THE BELLS ARE RINGING IN HARIDWAR

— THREE NOVELLAS —

Praise for *The Bells Are Ringing in Haridwar*

'Mukundan's *The Bells Are Ringing in Haridwar*, when it came out in Malayalam, conversed with a generation that was confused by life and its lack of certainties. This was the period of existentialist modernity. The writer's experiments in that genre of literature impressed the readers by their simplicity and accessibility. Mukundan indeed signalled a new wave in the aesthetics of Malayalam literature. The Mahe stories in this collection are immensely rewarding and bristling with life.'

N.E. Sudheer

'Mukundan's latest offering in translation is a collection of three novellas – the eponymous long novella and two short ones. But these are not new stories; on the contrary they are pretty old ones written in the late 1960s and early 70s. They have been introduced to the English-reading public some fifty years later in an interesting translation by Prema Jayakumar.

'[Haridwar] is a tale of harsh reality, of the consequences of drugs, and amplifies the striking contrast between what is considered sacred and what is profane.

'Mukundan manages to spin a good yarn that has us turning the pages. The author's overall narrative tapestry is rich with subtlety, a fine sense of humour, and has been wonderfully translated by Prema Jayakumar.'

The Book Review

'The novel which was way ahead of its time was criticized for its glorification of drug usage and the way of life which was considered immoral ... Rooted in reality the novel speaks of places and people, and lends a hand to step out of the frame to see the picture better. The translation releases it from the space it has been confined to helping the ideas and language transcends time and place and reaches a wider readership.'

DCB News, DC News Portal

Shortlisted for the Valley of Words Award 2020 for translation

The Bells Are Ringing in Haridwar

— THREE NOVELLAS —

M. MUKUNDAN

TRANSLATED FROM THE MALAYALAM BY

PREMA JAYAKUMAR

RATNA BOOKS

HARPERPERENNIAL

An Imprint of HarperCollins *Publishers*

First published as *Haridwaril Mani Muzhangunnu*, 1972; *Nagnanaya Thampuran*, 1989; *Savithriyute Aranhanam*, 1992 in Malayalam in India
First published in English in India by Ratna Sagar P. Ltd. 2019
This edition co-published in India in 2026
by
Harper Perennial
An imprint of HarperCollins *Publishers* India
Cyber City, Building 10-A, Gurugram, Haryana-122002, India
www.harpercollins.co.in
and
Ratna Sagar P. Ltd.
Virat Bhavan, Mukherjee Nagar Commercial Complex
Delhi 110009, India
www.ratnabookseries.wordpress.com

2 4 6 8 10 9 7 5 3 1

P-ISBN: 978-93-6989-176-4

Printed and bound at
Nutech Print Services Pvt. Ltd.

FSC
www.fsc.org
MIX
Paper | Supporting responsible forestry
FSC® C195953

This book is printed on FSC® certified paper which ensures responsible forest management.

HarperCollins *Publishers*, Macken House, 39/40 Mayor Street Upper, Dublin 1, D01 C9W8, Ireland

Contents

The Bells Are Ringing in Haridwar

One

Mussoorie, Shimla, Nainital…
Señor Herozi said.

Friday was a holiday because it was Independence Day. Saturday and Sunday were holidays as usual. Three days off in a row. Instead of making him happy, this scared him a bit. How would he spend these three days? Perhaps he could go out of town. But that was another problem. Where could he go? There were very few places left where Ramesh Panikkar could spend three days.

Jaisalmer, Khajuraho, Ajanta, Bhuvaneswar…

The white man continued.

Ramesh had already been to Mussoorie, Shimla and Nainital. He had wandered among the sun-baked ruins of Jaisalmer. He knew the sculptures of Khajuraho and the murals of Ajanta and Ellora in intimate detail. The walls of Khajuraho with their relief sculptures were the walls of his mind. The heat that rose from the sands of Jaisalmer was the heat of his soul. The flower-filled valleys of Kashmir were the dreams his heart held.

'Señor, suggest some other places please.'

Herozi put his feet up on the table and started scratching

his beard. He was thinking of another list.

'How about sacred places?' He stopped scratching his beard and looked at Ramesh.

'No problem.'

'Kasi?'

He'd never been to Kasi. But was it possible to go there and return in just three days? Kasi was far away. The distance from Yamuna to Ganga was huge.

'Fly there.' Herozi suggested.

If you flew, three days were sufficient. But then, there was another problem. Did he have the money? He would need at least a thousand rupees. He wouldn't be able to manage on less. He could ask Herozi and he would give. He had given a lot earlier too.

'What do you say?'

'I don't mind.'

The white man pressed down the intercom button and spoke, 'Check if there are any flights to Benares either on Thursday evening or Friday.'

Within five minutes, the reply came from the reception desk, 'No seats for either of the days.'

All flights were booked since it was a weekend. What next? The white man shook his legs on top of the table and continued to think. Ramesh also thought, his face buried in his hands. They were searching for a place on earth where one could spend three free days.

'Haridwar,' Ramesh sat up straight. 'I'm going to Haridwar, Señor.'

'That's good!'

The white man was happy. He lowered his legs from the

table, opened the cigarette tin and held it towards Ramesh. They lighted a cigarette each. He would still be travelling from Yamuna to Ganga. But it was not as far as Benares. It was only seven or eight hours by train.

Señor Herozi had seen Haridwar earlier. When the white man went on pilgrimages to Benares and Triveni, the confluence of the Ganga, Yamuna and Saraswati, the Indian, Ramesh, went in search of resorts and other places of pleasure. When Delhi froze in winter, Ramesh sought warm places. When sandstorms blew over Delhi, he would pick up his warm clothes and seek cold places. That was how Mall Road in Shimla became as familiar to him as Curzon Road in Delhi. And yet, he had forgotten the nearby Haridwar. Oh, the city of Prajapati Daksha, forgive me!

Friday, Saturday, Sunday – three days were plenty. He would be able to see whatever there was to see.

'Have you made up your mind?' Herozi caressed the golden sideburns that grew down his cheeks.

'Yes.'

'No changes?'

'No.'

'Well.'

So, one problem was solved. He had a plan of escape from the boredom of holidays. He could not imagine staying away from the office for three days. Going to the office was a part of his escapism. As he sat amidst his papers, listening to the rhythmic beat of the teleprinters, time was forgotten. As he translated words, sentences and paragraphs, he escaped from the curse of boredom. If the office did not exist, Ramesh's life would have been a desert. His mind was in Haridwar now, the

Haridwar in which echoed the Skandapurana, Padmapurana and Sivapurana. The Haridwar of Prajapati Daksha and that of Siva, the lord of Daksha. The Haridwar of Sati Devi, Manasa Devi and Anjana Devi. The Haridwar of Sage Dattatreya. The Haridwar of the seven divine sages…

'Make sure you return to Delhi by Monday,' the white man reminded him. His work could not go on if Ramesh were absent.

'I'll return on Sunday night, Señor. Is that enough?'

'Yes,' the white man nodded.

Every Monday evening, there was chess too. Ramesh had reached the semi-finals in the Delhi State Championship. Maybe he would even become the champion. Who knows? Ramesh Panikkar was champion in every game he played – chess, tennis, carrom…

There was always a lot of work at the office. The sahib who did not know how to write error-free English needed his help all the time. He wrote everything in Spanish. Each word had to be translated. If the translator was absent from the office the white man did not have an existence. Ramesh was his tongue. The white man's tongue was red like a dog's. Was Ramesh that tongue? He imagined his body was soaked in the white man's spit; a prisoner in the mouth of Señor Herozi, held back by his tobacco-darkened teeth.

The thought made Ramesh laugh. His own teeth were white and well-shaped, fit for a dentist's billboard.

'You have your father's teeth,' his mother would say. Where were his father's teeth now? They must have melted or exploded in the pyre. He realized he had no idea what happened to teeth after the body was cremated.

'Do you need anything?' Señor Herozi asked as he left the office in the evening. The question alluded to the need for cigarettes or whisky or something of that sort. There were five or six packs of the expensive Philips Morris at home. The bottle from the duty-free shop had not yet been opened.

'I don't need anything, Señor.'

The white man gave Ramesh not just whisky and cigarettes, he gave him many other things. They had often slept on either side of the same woman. But Ramesh was no longer interested in whisky. Instead he now used bhang. And charas instead of cigarettes. He was bored with alcohol and tobacco. What about women? He could use bhang in place of alcohol and charas in place of tobacco. But what could he use instead of women? There were only women in place of women in this world!

He collected his tobacco tin and pipe and the cheque book from his desk. The bank must have closed by now. Never mind. He could give a cheque to Mr Khosla, his landlord, and get some cash from him. Khosla's cupboard was always full of notes.

Normally, he would get out of the office with an overcast mind. He would just get out aimlessly. But this evening, he had an aim – to spend a couple of days in the land of Daksha Prajapati and Dattatreya. He walked through the broad streets of Chanakyapuri, past the red shadow of the Chinese Embassy, hands in his pockets, head full of pictures of Haridwar. He had heard about the Brahmakund and the temple of Manasa Devi that stood on the hilltop. He was going to see all that now. He would search through the nooks and corners of Haridwar, he would wander endlessly. Let his footsteps fall in Haridwar too. These footprints were all that he had in life. Ramesh walked past the huge buildings that seemed to be reaching for the sky. The walk that started from the womb and went on to the pyre. A funeral pyre must be getting ready somewhere on this earth for him too. A bundle of firewood and a matchstick must surely be waiting for him somewhere.

Recently, Ramesh had started thinking about death as never before. He had woken up that day too with a nightmare about death. He had gone to office with the bitter aftertaste of that nightmare in his mouth.

In response to the usual 'Buenos dias, amigo' that morning, he had said, 'I hear the footsteps of death, Señor.'

'Does death have feet? Ha, ha, ha!' The white man's thick cheeks shook with laughter. 'Are we born just to die?'

'We live so that we can die. Don't you know that there is no life, if there is no death?'

'There will be life even if there is no death. If death does not exist it will be only death that vanishes.'

When Suja rang up, he had told her too, 'Suja, I hear the footsteps of death.'

Her reply was, 'Those are my footsteps.'

There were only cars on the road. One couldn't see any pedestrians. The people of Chanakyapuri had wheels in place of feet. He could see the red faces of Russians in some of the cars. The yellow faces of the Chinese. Japanese with their squashed noses. And Negros with the beauty of the night. He walked and walked until he was out of the posh locality, the address of most embassies.

Suja had a painting class today. Otherwise, she would have

been waiting at the reception desk at his office by 5 o'clock. What did it matter whether she was with him or not? The fire of loneliness burnt hotter in the company of others. Reaching Ring Road, he did not feel like walking any further. He hailed a taxi from the taxi stand at the corner.

The taxi driver turned on the meter and looked at him.

'Seedha chalo.' (Go straight ahead)

Despite giving the direction to the driver, he had no idea where he wanted to go. There were many places he could visit, a lot of people he could look up. He could go to the Defence Pavilion and see the new play by Yatrik. He could go to the Club and play chess. He could go for a swim at the pool. Or he could ring up some girlfriend and sit under the open sky in the Rambler Restaurant. In spite of all these possibilities, it was as though he did not have anything to do.

He could go back home. A home was a womb. In its softness, in its moistness, in its warmth, he could bury his face between his knees and sleep.

'South Extension.'

The taxi driver accelerated now that he had clear instructions. The vehicle now had a definite goal, unlike the endless Ring Road, along which it was moving, that did not have a beginning or an end. If one traversed this road that circled the city, one could reach the exact point from where one had started. He thought of something else then. Why not tell the driver to go straight instead? He could sit for one or two hours in the taxi and just go around the city.

The taxi slowed down in front of the market at South Extension.

'Go straight.'

The vehicle went faster. Ramesh took out a small bundle of charas from the back pocket of his trousers. There was a technique of preparing charas. You took two matchsticks and held the charas firmly between the two. After that, you took another matchstick, struck it and held the flame under the charas . . . When the three matchsticks flared together, smoke rose from the charas. He rubbed the warm charas hard in his palm until it was powdered and filled his pipe with this and tobacco. The sound of a snake opening its mouth. In the meantime the taxi had reached Srinivasapuri. The driver turned around and looked at him.

'Straight.'

As he sat veiled by the thin, pale smoke of the charas, Ramesh wandered back into his past. As he went back twenty-six years, he could see his mother's womb. Red walls veined damply with blue. The damp, red darkness surrounded him. He lay head down in that darkness. The taxi moved along the deserted banks of the Yamuna. Azad Market, Kishanganj, Sarai Rohilla and Kirti Nagar were all left behind. Finally, they reached the place they had started from and the taxi halted.

'Saab,' the taxi driver tried to wake him up.

The pipe had burnt out. Ramesh rubbed his eyes and looked around. There is a place between death and life. Ramesh was in that space now. The charas he had bought for a rupee at Yusuf Sarai the previous day had cleared the way to the womb and the testicles. He got out of the taxi and took out three ten-rupee notes and refused the change. The taxi driver was obviously pleased. He folded his hands in thanks and withdrew.

The neon light streamed down like rain. Young girls with saris worn below the navel wandered around, nibbling at ice creams. A band was belting out songs in the Shagufa restaurant. Ramesh walked home through the magical world of colours and sounds. He switched on the air conditioner in his bedroom. The coolness spread like snow. He switched on his tape recorder. The sweet resonance of the sitar. He did not feel like eating anything. He had not eaten anything in the afternoon either. Still, he did not feel hungry. He pulled up the easy chair and lay on it. The intoxication of charas, hunger, the coolness, the sound of the sitar!

His eyes closed.

Two

Ramesh woke up. Manasa Devi and the Brahma Kund were calling out to him. He opened his eyes, thinking of Haridwar. His brain was filled with Haridwar. Why was he thinking so much about Haridwar? He had travelled a lot in the past four-five years. His heart had never beaten fast at the thought of a place like this. What had happened to his belief that the whole world was his oyster?

Just before the trip to Madrid, he had spent the whole day at the Club, playing cards and smoking charas. The flight was at eight-thirty in the evening. It was past seven when he got out of the Club. He went home and stuffed clothes and toiletries randomly into his suitcase and went to the airport – with all the ease of someone travelling from Kottayam to Kollam. He did not think about the flight, about Spain, or about the hard work that was waiting for him. His mind was engaged with the idea of using Mao's thoughts on the problems of chess.

Señorita Agino Herozi and Suja Mehra were waiting for him at the airport.

'Where were you?'

'I'm a little late, Señorita.'

'You've taken drugs, haven't you?' Señor Herozi's face showed anger.

'I was trying to apply Mao's thoughts to the problems of chess,' he lowered his voice and whispered to Suja. They had to run over the tarmac towards the plane.

But today, going to Haridwar, which was so near Delhi, Ramesh could not think of charas or chess. Haridwar had invaded his mind. Flames he had never seen were rising in his mind, and bells he had never heard were ringing in his ears. Was Haridwar calling out to him?

He threw off his duvet and sat up in the bed. The room was as cold as the inside of a refrigerator. He extended his hand to switch off the air conditioner. The machine stopped with a start and a tremble. When he pulled aside the curtains, a grey darkness entered the room. The concrete buildings nearby were palely visible. The world of concrete. The world of concrete troubled him. He had gone to his village during his last break to escape from the imprisonment of concrete. There was no concrete in his village. Instead there were coconut trees. There were only coconut trees wherever his eyes fell. He felt disturbed by the coconut trees. This feeling of disturbance – it was with him all the time. When he was in the village the coconut trees disturbed him. When he was in the city it was the concrete.

'I'll get rid of this disturbance of yours,' his mother's face had had a secret smile when she said that. He had accompanied her down the fields, wearing a white shirt and with his feet bare.

'Sit here,' his mother said, sitting down when they reached the culvert. He sat near her like an obedient child.

'What's the cause of your sorrow, child?'

'I don't know.'

'Don't you trust your mother?'

'How can you say that?'

'Then tell me.'

His mother had taken his hand and put it on her lap. Thin hands with a lot of hair. He had no secrets in his life that his mother did not know about. She knew that he used charas and bhang and that there were girls in his life. He always talked freely with her.

'Won't you tell me?' Her voice had been soft. She could see his lack of hope and his pain. She could also see that his health was being destroyed. She had wept over his letters. What was the reason for all this?

'Tell me, Ramesh, don't upset me like this.'

'I don't have any particular sorrow, mother. Perhaps that is the cause of my sorrow.'

Ramesh looked at his mother's face. Would she be able to digest what he was saying? His mother was as educated as he was. She also had more experience in life. Add to it the fact that she had been teaching for nearly two decades in a college that was famous for having produced a huge number of intellectuals. No, his mother would have no problem in understanding what he was saying.

'So, I guess your problem is metaphysical.'

His mother got up from the culvert and added, 'And your sorrow can only be cured by another sorrow, right?'

Yes, only sorrow can save me. If only my chest could be invaded by tuberculosis…if only my throat had cancer…if only my eyes burst…

'Do you go to the temple, mother?'

'No, I don't.'

'You must go once for my sake. Go and pray to god that I catch tuberculosis.'

His mother had not replied, but had held his hand tight and walked on.

He continued excitedly, 'Or cancer. If I got cancer of the throat and was struggling to swallow even water, I think I would be happy. Go today itself to the temple, amma, and pray that I may get cancer.'

Ramesh knelt before his mother and buried his face in her hands.

'Ramesh, don't act mad.'

His mother lifted him up. They walked silently along the bank of the river. After a little while, Ramesh saw her wiping her eyes with the edge of the white sari she wore.

The next day too, mother and son wandered across the fields and by the river.

'I'll let you go on your destructive path for another year. After that, I'll straighten you out.'

The next year, his mother would retire from work. She had three desires to fulfil after that.

'I'll get you married.'

'And then?'

'I'll come to Delhi and stay with the two of you.'

'And what's the third wish?'

'That's quite simple. I want a lot of books to read till I die.'

'Why do you want to come to Delhi?'

'To feed you and bathe you and put you to sleep.'

'Won't she do all that for me?'

'Suppose she's also like you?' His mother smiled.

'Why must you feed me and bathe me and put me to sleep? Don't I bathe now? Don't I sleep?'

'You won't understand what I'm saying, Ramesh.'

His mother held his hand tight and walked beside the river. Her language was not English or Malayalam or French. It was a mother's language.

'Do you believe in love, mother?'

Ramesh laid stretched out on the bed, smoking. His mother sat on the bed and caressed his hair and forehead. He had his father's forehead, the same nose…

'Do you believe in love, mother?'

'What kind of question is that, child? You're all I have in this world. Why don't you understand that?'

'You didn't answer my question.'

'What question?'

'Whether you believe in love.'

'I do.'

Ramesh lighted another cigarette and blew the smoke towards his mother's face. She did not turn her face away. His father used to do the same thing.

'There is nothing called love.'

'A lot of people have said that, Ramesh.'

'There are only relationships. You love me because I'm your son. If not, you wouldn't love me, you probably wouldn't speak even one word to me if we met somewhere. If you saw me suddenly, you might ask me, "Who are you? Where are you from?"'

His mother did not say anything, but continued to caress his hair silently.

'Can you prove that there is love?'

'What's difficult about that? The lion is a cruel animal, it kills any creature that comes before it. Even if it sees an elephant that is much larger than itself, it roars with anger and attacks it. And does this cruel animal roar when it sees its own child? It does not eat it, but instead plays with it. Why does this happen?'

His mother continued with an air of victory, 'That, Ramesh, is love.'

Ramesh felt like laughing when he heard his mother's argument. He said, 'The lion does not kill and eat its cub, not because it loves it, but because it is its child. This is not love, mother, it is a relationship.'

'I can't argue with you,' his mother gave up and laughed with him.

He had stayed only a fortnight. When he was in Delhi, he felt like going to the village. As soon as he reached the village, he would be in a hurry to return to the city. His mother was with him like a shadow, all the time he was at home. She would heat the water for him to bathe, feed him till he could eat no more, come and cover him when he slept at night. Ramesh was not happy in the village. It was not that he missed charas and female company. He wasn't happy in Delhi either even though he got all that there.

He remembered a night in the village. Sleep had refused to come even after midnight. He twisted and turned in bed and then paced the room till his legs ached. There was the silence of a desert in his mind then. Emptiness. He went to the kitchen to get a drink of water and saw his mother's kitchen knife on the table. He picked up the knife and cut his finger – first one and then two fingers. When a lot of blood flowed out and pain flamed, his mind quietened down and he felt sleepy…

His mother was happy during the days he visited. She looked after Ramesh as though he were a small child. She had no one else whom she could bathe and feed and put to sleep.

Three

His mother wanted to go to Haridwar and Benares. She was already making plans to see all those holy places when she came to stay with him in Delhi. I shall fulfil your wishes, mother. I'll go to the temples at Haridwar and pray for you. Daksheswar, here I come, to prepare the way for my mother's arrival.

The alarm on his wrist watch sounded. It was five-thirty. There was a pale light over the concrete buildings around. It had been a long time since he saw the sun rise! He normally slept very late in the night and by the time he woke up the sun would be blazing brightly. Today was a good day. A good day when he had seen the sun rise. The good day when he was going to Haridwar. He stood near the window and brushed his teeth. He then stripped off all his clothes and stood naked under the shower. He had already shaved at night and so did not have that to do. He packed his suitcase – trousers, shirts, night clothes, after-shave lotion, eau de cologne, pipes, a tin of tobacco, sleeping pills. One thing was missing: charas. He had to buy it on the way to the station. There was no way he was taking a chance of trying to find a dealer in Haridwar.

He was very hungry. He had not eaten anything the

previous day. He opened the refrigerator and looked inside. There were eggs, but he did not feel like cooking them. There were a couple of slices of salami in a corner of the freezer. He made a sandwich with those and ate it, finishing off with a cup of tea. He was still hungry but good to go. He dressed in a half-sleeved cotton shirt with red checks and trousers suitable for a journey. He carried the suitcase out and locked the room. Daksha Prajapati, Manasa Devi, Dattatreya, here I come.

'What are you up to?' asked Rahul Khosla, pacing the veranda clad in a shiny dressing gown, accompanied by his dog.

'I'm going to Haridwar, Rahul Bhaiya.'

'Planning to renounce the world?'

Nalini Khosla came out too. As the last buttons of the night gown had been left undone, the edge of the underskirt could be seen. And beneath that, her fair feet.

'Didi, what would you like me to bring you from Haridwar?'

'A conch shell.'

She must be planning to keep it in the display cabinet.

'And for you, Rahul Bhaiya?'

'A little gangajal, water from the Ganges.'

His voice was unsteady. Rahul Khosla had become a heart patient in his youth. He put his hand through the open gown and rubbed his chest. There was a moment's silence.

Nalini Didi broke the silence and asked, 'Are you going alone to Haridwar?'

Ramesh never went anywhere alone.

'I'm alone in this world, Didi.'

Ramesh walked out, carrying the suitcase. He had to go to Yusuf Sarai first. Charas was a forbidden substance. One could not get it just anywhere. It was dangerous to carry too much of it as well. It was usually bought in secret places as small pills and often hidden in socks. Last winter he had bought a hundred rupees' worth of charas from a hippie. So, winter had passed pleasurably.

He stopped the taxi at Yusuf Sarai. Nathu scratched his bum and got up. He smiled with his eyes and greeted him without words. The merchants of charas spoke with their eyes and not with their mouth.

'Dus – ten.' Would ten pills be enough? If not, he could find out if it was available in Haridwar. He paid Nathu, took the bundle from him and signalled to the driver to move.

Nathu would not have given ten pills at one go if the customer had been anyone else. He knew Ramesh Babu very well. Before Nathu got into selling charas, he dealt in the illicit arrack called 'jagadari'. And pimping. Those days Ramesh Babu was a regular customer for both commodities. Nathu and Ramesh Babu were old acquaintances.

The taxi sped towards the railway station. The hippies who slept in the verandas of Connaught Place were beginning to wake up. The area in front of the station was as crowded as ever, even though it was early morning. Paying off the driver, he walked into the station, carrying his suitcase. Trains panted and roared on the many tracks. The air was black with smoke. Hot steam rose from the railway engines. Mussoorie Express was standing at the designated platform. Ramesh saw Suja standing beside the train, leaning against a pillar. There was a small suitcase at her feet. When she saw Ramesh at a distance, a smile appeared in her eyes, her cheeks and her lips.

Four

The Mussoorie Express moved over the rails like a tamed beast, roaring and panting in turn. Passing the tangled railway yards, the train reached Nigambodh Ghat. The funeral pyres on the banks of the Yamuna never died down. Even before one died down, the next started burning. The clear water reflected the flames of the pyres at a distance. The thick walls of the Red Fort were now behind them.

'Farewell Red Fort, farewell Jama Masjid,' Suja said, extending her hands through the window and waving. Ramesh took out his pipe and the tin of tobacco. Sending out streams of smoke from the pipe, he too looked out. The doves were flying over the Yamuna. These were the doves that flocked outside the Gurudwara in Chandni Chowk in search of grains. The train was now on the long bridge over the Yamuna.

'Farewell, farewell!' Suja murmured, looking at Delhi which was growing more distant behind them. 'Give us leave to be away for three days. We shall come back after that. We shall sit on the steps of the Jama Masjid and speak in riddles. We shall wander in the shade of the Red Fort again. Dear city, forget us for three days.'

For the next three days, Haridwar would be their Delhi, and the Brahmakund would serve for Connaught Place. The train had crossed the bridge by now. In the afternoon it would be the bridge across the Ganga that they would cross. The journey from Yamuna to Ganga. Ramesh sat leaning against the back rest, sending out smoke through his mouth and nostrils. There were not many passengers as it was a first-class compartment. There was only one other passenger, a white man, besides Suja and Ramesh. He kept wiping his eyes and nose with a handkerchief.

'He'll rape you if he gets a chance. You'd better be careful, Suja.'

Suja looked at the white man and giggled. He was a thin man with unruly hair. He seemed disturbed by Suja's laughter and turned his face away.

'Doesn't he look as though he's just got up from under the bridge in Paris? Like Clochard?'

Suja started giggling again, looking at the man. His face looked as though he was swallowing something bitter. Poor man. Ramesh pulled hard at his pipe. It was almost dead.

'Suja!'

'Umm?' She responded, not taking her eyes off the man's face.

'I was imagining the rape scene.'

'Umm.'

Suja did not move her eyes from the face of the white man. The man got up and she started laughing aloud at the same moment. He muttered something to himself and went and sat in a seat far away from them. Ramesh knocked out the ashes from the dead pipe and started cleaning it. Suja laughed to herself for some more time at the thought of having beaten the white man. She then looked out through the window.

'I'm feeling sad. I miss Delhi.'

Suja was born and brought up in Delhi. And so, it was difficult for Suja Mehra to part from Delhi. Ramesh did not feel the pangs of parting. He had not been sad even when he left his village and came to Delhi for the first time. His place was not Kerala or Delhi or any other place. This earth was Ramesh's own place. He was a traveller who journeyed through the dark. In between, he lost his way sometimes and reached inside some womb. He had visited so many wombs within this time!...

'Suja, would you be able to prepare a pyre for me?'

'Won't the electric crematorium do?'

'One needs a death certificate to go there.'

'There is that chandaal who attends to the cremation ceremonies there. One can always bribe him.'

The kakhi-clad chandaal whose eyes were the colour of the pyre and whose body smelled of corpses was called Sriram. Some time back, Ramesh had spent a whole day in the crematorium. He had stood and looked at the hearses come and go. He saw the priests do the final rites, putting rice and wicks in the corpses' mouths. That was the first time he had seen so many corpses. If one gave him a lot of money, would Sriram burn him alive? There was nothing that money could not buy, after all. Ramesh started seeing himself burning on a pyre. Sriram would place him on the steel plate. The priests would put cooked rice and lighted wicks in his mouth. Then Sriram would pull the levers of the machine that were fixed to the wall and push him into the oven. Even before entering it fully, his hair and clothes would burn. Within seconds the body would become a burnt mass of flesh. Then the bones would burst. Finally, when he became just a handful of ashes, Sriram would open the back of the oven and sweep out the ashes. Someone would put those ashes in an earthen pot, put some more earth over them and send it floating in the Yamuna.

Suja took out a flask and a package from her bag. She poured out tea from the flask into paper cups.

'What's in the package?'

'Guess.'

'Sandwiches.'

Suja looked at Ramesh's face wonderingly. He too was rather surprised. How had he known that?

She offered him a sandwich.

'I don't want it. I had one in the morning.'

'Wasn't that a frozen salami sandwich?'

'How did you know that?' Ramesh looked at Suja's face in wonder. She too was shocked. How had she known that?

'Shall I give him a piece too?'

The white man who now sat some distance away was glancing at them intermittently.

'Let the poor man alone, Suja. Give me one.'

They ate the sandwiches and drank the tea. He could not taste the tomatoes in the sandwich. All that charas he had taken in had destroyed his taste buds. After a while would his eyes lose the ability to distinguish colours? Would his ears forget sounds and his nose forget smells? Suja put the empty flask back into the bag. That bag of hers was large enough to hold a child. Closing the bag and putting her hands around her knees, she asked, 'What shall we do now?'

She found the answer herself, 'We can sit and think.'

They could think. But think about what? He was fed up of thinking. He had been thinking for twenty-six years now. If only he could sit for one moment without thinking of anything – he could not help wishing.

'Ramesh, what are you thinking about?'

'How one could sit without thinking. What about you?'

'Me? I don't know.'

'That's a lie.'

'It's true, Ramesh!'

After a while Ramesh asked again, 'What are you thinking about now?'

'I was thinking of my mother.'

'What's there to think about her?'

She pulled up her feet on the seat and sat with her knees raised and her chin on her knees. She adjusted her sari to cover her small fair feet. Suja's mother was not opposed to her daughter marrying Ramesh. But she did object to her daughter going to his room often and to wandering here and there with him. When Suja had asked for permission to go with him to Haridwar, Ramesh had been sitting in the drawing room. 'Ask your daddy.'

Ramesh had noticed how her voice had changed. He had feared that she would object and his Haridwar programme would collapse. Suja's daddy was not in Delhi. He was always on tour.

'But, Daddy is not here.'

'Ask him when he comes.'

Suja's mother had glowered with displeasure. Although

she had travelled widely and was the wife of a senior government official, she had not lost her old-fashioned prejudices. She continued to be the daughter of the wheat fields of Punjab. Suja was just the opposite. She was a hippy before the world knew hippies. She had made a hero of Che Guevara even before he became popular with the hip crowd. Now that everyone idolized him, she had gotten over her hero worship. She was looking for a new incarnation, the arrival of a sort of super-Che now.

Her mother did not give her permission.

'I'll go whether you give me permission or not. I'm not going with some stranger, but with Ramesh.'

'You can go on trips with him after you get married.'

'I'll go.'

'Let me see you do that.'

Suja got ready for the journey without her mother's permission. Her mother watched angrily as she got up early in the morning, bathed, got dressed and made sandwiches. She could not bear it when her daughter wore a blue voile sari and marked her forehead with a big bindi.

'You wanton girl! Let your father get back.'

The driver brought the car out of the garage. Suja, who had stepped out of the house, came back and put her arms around her mother. When she showered her mother's face with its faint smell of supari with kisses, her mother turned her face away.

'The puritan in you will never die.'

'When does your daddy get back?'

'He should be back on Monday or Tuesday. We'll ask his permission for me to go to Haridwar then.'

She smiled at her mother. She had faith in her father. He'd never failed in understanding his daughter.

'Will they complain to the police that I've kidnapped you?'

'We've eloped, haven't we?'

'The same thing. Elopement is just kidnapping oneself.'

She started paying attention to his fingers. His fingers were moving over her toes and her heels. Only he could caress her skin like this. Those magical fingers of his moved upwards and touched her navel above the sari, the back of her neck, and her hair. Her head, with its faint smell of shampoo, reclined on his chest.

'See if there are any lice.'

His charas-stained fingers wandered through her hair. She started dozing off in the hypnotic trance created by those circling fingers.

'Suja!'

'Umm?'

'What are you thinking about?'

'About Regis Debray. And you, Ramesh?'

'I'll think of Debray too.'

Ramesh's thoughts turned from lice to guerrilla warfare. His mind now held the picture of Debray's fiery eyes and thick moustache.

'Did I tell you about my discovery?'

'What discovery?'

'Debray once said that the city would turn the proletariat into bourgeoisie, didn't he?'

'Yes, he did.'

'Didn't he also say that villages would turn the bourgeoisie into the proletariat?'

'Yes.'

'If so, the Russian revolution was brought about by the bourgeoisie.'

Suja looked at him, bewildered.

'If what Debray said was true, the proletariat of Petrograd would have become bourgeoisie, wouldn't they? Petrograd is a city.'

'That's true,' Suja nodded in agreement.

'It's not my discovery. It owes its existence to the power of charas.'

It was when he was smoking charas that he had discovered that Mao's thoughts could be applied to chess. At the start of the game, all the pieces would rush forward in a flood of moves. The enemy would be startled and be destroyed in that startled state. If the enemy was intelligent, a line of defence would be formed, and the attack would be met by a counter-attack. Then he would withdraw.

'When the enemy attacks, you retreat.'

The train passed Ghaziabad and Modinagar and stopped at Meerut. Ramesh and Suja got out of the train and walked up and down the platform.

'Will you buy me a surahi?'

An old man was sitting on the platform selling surahis, those long-necked jars for keeping water.

'A surahi? What for?'

'I want one.'

She squatted before the earthen pots. There were surahis of all shapes and sizes. Suja chose a surahi with a lion's head for a mouth.

'Pay him, Ramesh.'

He paid the money. She stood for a moment, enjoying the beauty of the surahi. Then she walked towards an area where there were not many people, and threw the surahi hard on the ground.

Looking at the scattered pieces of the surahi, she said, 'I'm returning to my childhood.'

The moment they got into the compartment, the train hooted and left Meerut Cantonment.

'Do you want to return to your childhood, Ramesh?'

'I'm more interested in getting to my old age.'

He did not have to worry about that, she said, as he was set on the path to old age with the help of charas and starvation.

The train moved past villages and small towns and fields and the slopes of hills, towards Roorkee. River Yamuna and the city of Delhi on its banks were far away now.

'Ramesh, what are you thinking about now?'

'About your mother. What if she throws you out of the house when you get back to Delhi?'

'I'll come to Y-14.'

Y-14 was Ramesh's residence. It held a bed for him to sleep, an air conditioner to cool the room in summer and heat the room in winter, a tape recorder to listen to music, a telephone to speak to his friends. 'Y-14 welcomes you.'

'By the time I get back, mummy would have got over her anger.'

Suja's mother was quick to anger, but she got over it just as quickly. She was a nice person. Suja was the only child. She had been born after placing an offering of five thousand and one rupees in the golden temple at Amritsar. She had been bought from the gods.

'I can hear Bhageeratha's chariot,' Ramesh said when the train reached Roorkee.

He could see the Ganga flow, all eddies, through the city. The people of the city were bathing at the ghats. The train left Roorkee and moved towards Haridwar. The roar of the train now had the tune of mantras being chanted. Was the smoke that rose from the train, the smoke from the sacrificial fires? Ramesh felt that he could hear the sound of conches from the valley of the Shivalik mountains. He became silent.

The Mussoorie Express reached Haridwar, finally.

Five

Suja patted down her hair that was flying here and there and got down from the train. A porter came running. After handing over the suitcases to him, Ramesh looked around to see if they had forgotten anything. The cigarette butts that he had discarded, the wrappers of the chocolates that Suja had eaten, the paper cups that she had left there after drinking tea – there was nothing other than these in the compartment. He too got down from the train. He stood on the soil of Haridwar.

Ramesh looked around him. His eyes held his desire to discover Haridwar. His nostrils widened to take in the smell of Haridwar. His ears opened wide to hear the sounds of Haridwar. What he saw was a small, dirty railway station. There was an old man selling bhaturas, deep-fried leavened bread, and spicy chickpeas. There was a fruit seller who pushed his cart filled with over-ripe fruits. Some beggars lay here and there on the benches and the floor, half-asleep in the heat of the day.

A gaggle of coolies crowded around the doors of the train greedily. Only four-five villagers had got down there other than Ramesh and Suja. They didn't have any suitcases, only bundles that they carried themselves. The walls of the platform were covered with advertisements. Most of them were film posters. Mumtaz, Sharmila Tagore, Mala Sinha, Shammi Kapoor . . . Were the walls of Haridwar also decorated with pictures of film stars? There wasn't a single picture of a god among them.

'The gods of Haridwar,' Ramesh pointed at the dancing Shammi Kapoor and the swimsuit-clad Mumtaz. One could see them wherever one went – on the streets of Delhi, on the walls of urinals, at bus stands.

'We need the film stars more than we need gods, Ramesh. They entertain us. Gods just frighten us, don't they?'

Suja was right. Gods had always troubled mankind. Shammi Kapoor and Mumtaz always entertained them. When Shammi Kapoor danced and Mumtaz sang in a swimsuit, the poor and the troubled forgot their poverty and troubles.

There was a path full of potholes leading from the station. It ended at a gate that opened out to the road. Cycle rickshaw-pullers, judka drivers and taxi drivers started crowding around them.

'Babuji, rickshaw.'

'Babuji, taxi.'

They surrounded Ramesh and Suja. Their eyes showed sadness and misery. Starving people with unshaven faces and uncombed hair. If only he could travel in all their taxis, judkas and rickshaws! If only he could satisfy all of them, Ramesh could not help wishing.

'Babuji, come with me. First class room, fan, attached bathroom . . .' This was a young man with green eyes, wearing a pair of trousers and a half-sleeved shirt. He must be the tout for some hotel. He looked at Ramesh and Suja greedily. By then touts of other hotels also reached them. They started arguing with each other and even pushing each other.

'Dafa ho jao,' yelled the porter who was carrying their suitcases. 'Get lost.'

As they got out of the crush, he asked, 'Shall I show you a hotel, Babuji?'

'Where is it?'

'It's on the Upar Sadak, the upper road.'

But where was this Upar Sadak?

'Is it near the ghat?'

'Yes, Babu.'

It would be good to stay in a hotel on the banks of the river. They could sit looking at the hypnotizing water of the river all the time. The music of the Ganga would be in their ears as they ate and slept. The porter walked along with their suitcases. Ramesh and Suja followed him, walking on the soil of Haridwar. The road was a narrow one, marked as though it had caught leprosy. On one side of the path stood the rickshaws like unknown corpses. On the other side of the path were narrow and dirty shop fronts. In front of the shops stood hawkers selling all sorts of eatables. As they walked, the touts of various hotels kept trying to get near them. The porter yelled at them and kept them at a distance.

Was this Haridwar? Ramesh asked himself. The touts who followed them like restless ghosts, the rickshaw-pullers who groaned and whined all around them, these narrow shops, this path with its wounded look – was this Haridwar?

'Suja, is this Haridwar?'

'Yes, Ramesh, we are at Haridwar.'

The hair that Suja had combed back had started coming loose and was falling on her cheeks.

'What is the name of this street?'

'It doesn't have a name, Madam.'

The porter pointed to a saffron-coloured building on the left and said, 'That's our hotel, Babu.'

A faded board hung in front of the hotel – Srigangaji Hotel. The hotel was on the first floor. The porter lowered the suitcases from his head and started climbing the steps holding them in his hands. The stairs were between a motor workshop and a tobacco and betel leaves shop. The steps were damp and had a terrible smell. They ended abruptly in an open space. Someone was sleeping on a charpoy there.

'Munimji, o munimji!'

The porter woke him. It was an old man. Ramesh felt like throwing up when he saw his face. On his right cheek he had a festering sore about the size of a rupee coin, filled with blood and pus. Flies were buzzing round it. It was a terrible sight. The porter murmured something in the old man's ear. Munimji picked up a set of keys from under his pillow and walked across the space.

'Munimji, it should be a first-class room. These people are from Delhi.'

The porter picked up the suitcases and followed Munimji. The old man opened the lock of a room. When he pushed open the door, they could hear the wing beats of bats from the other end. The room had no windows or cupboards. The walls were scarred and mildewed.

'This is the room.'

The porter unwound the cloth that had been tied around

his head and wiped the sweat from his face and neck. His eyes were anxious. A rusty fan hung from the ceiling. Ramesh tried switching on the fan. It did not move.

'There's no electricity at the moment, Babuji,' Munimji said, caressing his sore. It was obviously a lie.

'The toilet is there.' Munimji pointed out the toilet. The toilet and the bathroom were together. They could not even go near it, the smell was so bad. There were flies buzzing beyond the broken door.

'Munimji is a good person. You can trust him. He'll give you whatever help you want,' the porter continued to talk.

Munimji came with an oily ledger and asked, 'How many days will you stay, Babu?'

Ramesh did not reply. He took out two one-rupee notes from his pocket and put them on the charpoy before the porter. Picking up the suitcases, Ramesh started down the stairs.

'Babuji!' The porter cried out desperately.

He would have got a commission for bringing two customers to Munimji. That had vanished now. His desperate voice pierced Ramesh's ears like nails. Munimji kept muttering some curses.

'Give me one of the suitcases, I'll carry it,' Suja held out her hand for the suitcase.

Ramesh did not hand over the suitcases. He walked on with a burning cigarette between his lips and suitcases in either hands. Suja walked with him. Silence thickened between them. Munimji and his hotel lay like a sore in their minds.

'Babuji!' voices whined from either side of the street. They might be beggars or touts. There were rows of rentals on either side of the nameless street. Ramesh saw the board of a hotel at the junction where the road met the one from the railway station. Ramesh went towards it. Suja stood guard over the suitcases on the road.

'Come, come!'

Lalaji, the owner of the hotel, bowed when he saw Ramesh's looks and clothes. Ramesh glanced inwards. There was stagnant water in the corridor. The rooms were on either side of the corridor. Two breechclouts lay drying at the entrance of the corridor – both yellowed with urine.

'No good, Suja!'

'We'll stay at some charity place, Ramesh.'

If this was the state of the hotels, what would be the state of the dharmashalas – charity guest houses? Gita Dharmashala, Harihar Dharmashala, Yati Chaitanya Dharmashala, Gayatridevi Dharmashala, Sriganga Dharmashala, Gangotri Dharmashala – so many charity guest houses. You only had to pay twenty-five paise and they would give you six feet of space to lie in.

'Are you game?'

'No,' she smiled.

Buildings were piled up on either side of the Upar Sadak. The vendors of snacks yelled themselves hoarse. What was the difference between this Upar Sadak and the streets of Old Delhi? There was one difference. If the street had been in Delhi, it would have been called Nai Sadak or Gali Kasiram instead of Upar Sadak. Gali Kasiram must have changed its name and come and taken its place here. Old Delhi must have changed shape and become Haridwar.

'Ramesh, what are you thinking?

'Isn't this Haridwar our Old Delhi in a different form?'

Suja laughed aloud. She always found it easy to laugh. Some people are born to cry and others to laugh. This girl belonged to the second group.

They were near the Lalta Rao Bridge by now. The railings of the bridge were broken. What flowed beneath was not the Ganga, but a drain. He saw a hotel beyond the Police Station. At first glance, it seemed fairly clean.

'I'll sit here,' Suja sat on one of the suitcases.

'Tired?'

She did not reply, but smiled. Her face had become smaller with the long journey and then the walk in the sun. There were strands of hair sticking to her sweaty forehead and cheeks...

A young man in trousers and shirt and a tie stood up when he saw Ramesh. He showed him a room respectfully. The room had a carpeted floor, fans, cupboards, a table lamp, a bathtub in the bathroom. The young man started speaking about his hotel in excellent English. It had all the conveniences. The Post Office was nearby and there was a hospital close by too.

'Hospital? But, I'm quite all right!' Ramesh said.

The young man laughed aloud when he heard that. If Suja had been with them, she would have laughed even louder. Ramesh looked out. There she sat on the suitcase, at a distance in the street, with her chin on her palm.

'It's right in the middle of the city. Behind, you have the hills and Manasa Devi temple...', the young man went on.

'A good room. A bathroom with a bathtub. Come Suja,' Ramesh picked up the suitcases and walked to the hotel.

He liked the room and the bathroom. Suja's face held

the relief of having found a place finally. Was there such a shortage of good hotels in Haridwar?

'Suja, people don't come here to enjoy themselves. They come here to wash away their sins. Why would they need good hotels?'

When the young man came with the register, Ramesh wrote in it: Mr and Mrs Ramesh Panikkar, Tourists, Y-14, South Extension, New Delhi - 31. Visit of three days' duration. The young man took the register and went to get the keys to the room.

This was not the first time they were becoming husband and wife. They were a married couple in all the invitations that came from the United Sates Information Centre. They had also become husband and wife when they happened to stay for a couple of days in a hotel in Chandigarh.

'We're good actors!'

'One day, this acting will become the truth, Suja.'

'I'm waiting for the day.'

Suja was in a hurry for that day to arrive.

'Are you in a hurry, Ramesh?'

'I'm actually against the institution of marriage.'

He would often say that he did not like the prison created by those eight letters.

'In my eyes, a society that permits free sex is heaven.'

'But what about family life, Ramesh?'

'Can't a human being live without a family?'

'I want my daddy and mummy.'

'Suja, in the last count, there is no father, no mother, there is only man and woman. That means, you and me.'

A white-clad servitor came and picked up the suitcases.

'I am Avinash Arora,' the young man introduced himself. Suja and Ramesh walked after him to their room. The room was on the first floor. There was a small balcony outside the room, with a couple of cane chairs.

'You can sit here and look at Haridwar,' Arora told them.

Ramesh went out on to the balcony and looked out. What Arora said was true. You could see the Ganga in the distance.

'Something to drink?' Arora asked politely.

'A Coca Cola for me. Tea for Ramesh,' Suja replied.

Arora came with the Coca Cola and a waiter brought the tea. Suja placed the strainer over the cup and poured out the tea. She mixed the sugar and milk, stirred with a spoon and held it out to Ramesh.

'Gracias, Señorita.'

He thought of Señor Hirozi. What would he be doing now? Perhaps he was in the swimming pool at the Asoka Hotel. Or would he be in a daze induced by bhang? He had been taught the use of bhang by Ramesh. Ramesh remembered when Hirozi had taken bhang for the first time. It had no effect on him. He had taken two-hundred grams of ground bhang. Nothing happened even after three hours.

'Is this the wonderful bhang that you were going on and on about?' Señor Hirozi had made fun of him.

He took his car out and went to the swimming pool at the Asoka Hotel. Changing into swimming trunks, he dived into the pool. He later said that he had seen ten-thousand colours as he lay in water. If there had been no one else nearby, the sahib would have drowned in the colours.

'Anything else?' Arora asked politely.

'You may go.'

Arora was whistling as he went away. A smart young man. Suja and Ramesh were alone in the room now.

'Suja, do you like the room?'

'Do you need to ask?'

'Better than your room, isn't it?'

'What's wrong with my room?'

'Is your room airconditioned?'

She did not reply.

'Is there a Tibetan carpet in your room?'

'We aren't rich.'

'Who's this "we"?' Ramesh spread his legs out, leaned back against the chair and asked. 'You and me?'

'I'm going to take a bath,' she got up.

'Don't,' Ramesh said with his eyes shut. Sipping the hot tea, he continued, 'Don't bathe, let your hair be filled with lice. I'll cook them and eat them with my beer.'

She laughed even as she was opening the suitcase. She took out shampoo and a towel. And an underskirt.

'Suja, what all do you have in your suitcase? Are there sanitary towels in it?'

Her face reddened.

'Don't talk nonsense,' she shut the suitcase and got up. She undid her plaits. Her dark hair spread over her shoulders.

As she walked towards the bathroom, he asked, 'Shall I bathe you?'

'Gracias, Señor.'

Suja also knew a little bit of Hirozi's language. She went for her bath, humming under her breath. Ramesh sat alone, cigarette between his lips. I've finally reached Haridwar. After wandering for long in the deserts of bhang, after wandering in the forests of charas, after swimming through women, Haridwar, I've reached your presence. What's the end of this journey? Daksheswar, tell me, how far must I wander again?

He was tired after the journey and the walk in the sun. His thoughts broke as he lay there with his eyes shut. Sleep entered him through his ears and eyes like a thin stream of steam...

He opened his eyes to the intoxicating smell of a mixture of shampoo and wet hair. She was standing before the mirror with wet hair left loose. One end of a green sari was tucked into her underskirt. The rest of the sari lay trailing on the ground. The strap of her bra could be seen on her naked shoulder between her neck and the edge of the blouse.

'Don't you want to take a bath?' she asked with her eyes still on the mirror, as she combed her hair.

'No.'

'Planning to sleep?'

'No.'

'Then?'

'A charas trip. I feel like it.'

'You can't get charas here.' She turned her head as she said this happily. 'You can't get drugs and alcohol here. Don't you know that? Poor you!'

'But I've brought the stuff with me. Poor you!'

All intoxicants and meat and fish were banned in Haridwar. Who needed fish and meat anyway? But how could he survive without a piece of charas or a drop of bhang? These substances were a part of his life. Ramesh might be able to live without salt or water. But he could not survive even one day without charas or opium.

'Ramesh, will you do something for me?' Suja had asked once as they lay together damp in each other's sweat, her head on his chest.

'What is it?'

'Promise you'll do it. I'll tell you only then.'

'Tell me what it is first.'

She lay silent for a while. That was the day they had decided they would get married the next December in Delhi. His mother would come from Kerala during the Christmas vacation. It was a day they had been happy.

'Tell me, my dear.'

'Don't smoke charas. I don't like you smoking it. I can't stand it.'

'Poor girl!' He showered her with kisses.

'I'll do anything for you. I'll even stop breathing. Will that do?'

She did not say anything further. She still disliked his smoking charas. But whenever he asked her to, she bought the pills from Nathu in Yusuf Sarai. He had introduced her one day to the one-armed Nathu. Nathu thought she was Ramesh's wife. Nathu had said once that Suja was the only girl who came to him to buy charas.

'Do you know, Suja, Vyasa wrote the Mahabharata under the influence of narcotics. Probably bhang.'

'Why don't you add that Newton discovered gravity under the influence of bhang?' She laughed at him as she combed her hair.

How could anyone create a Kurukshetra without bhang? How can anyone imagine the trick of making arrows rain fire except under the influence of some psychedelic substance?

'All the sages were narcotic addicts. Or else they wouldn't have been able to sit on the sharp edge of a trident and meditate.'

These were arguments she listened to every day. Suja stood before the mirror and wore her sari properly.

'It is not right that narcotics are banned in Haridwar, which is the land of gods and sages.'

She put a green bindi on her forehead to match her sari.

'If you don't want to bathe, don't. But at least change your clothes.'

'I don't want to.' He would not bathe, he would not change his clothes.

'I'm fed up with you, Ramesh.'

'Will you do me a favour?'

'What?'

The pills of charas he'd bought in Yusuf Sarai in the morning were lying in the pocket of his trousers. He took out one.

'Please prepare this for me. The pipe is in the pocket of the suitcase.'

She knelt on the carpet and took out the pipe and the tobacco tin from the suitcase. She held the charas that had hardened into a stone-like consistency between two matchsticks and heated it with a lighted match. The charas would not powder well if it was not heated. She powdered the charas and filled the pipe with a mixture of tobacco and the powder.

'Here.'

He took the pipe from her. She knew the technique of filling the pipe well by now. She sat on one of the chairs with a book. She read quite a lot. He did not read much these days. The time for reading was over. It was now time for meditation. What was the point in reading so much? He now got to know about new books only when Suja spoke about them.

Ramesh went to the veranda, pulled the chair closer to the railings and sat on it. He lifted his legs and put them on the railing. This was the most comfortable position. He held the pipe between his teeth and called out, 'Suja, the matchbox.'

He'd forgotten to bring his lighter. She found a matchbox from somewhere. When he lighted the pipe, the indescribable perfume of charas spread over the veranda. This perfume could not be compared with any other perfume on earth. The smell that provoked him the most was Chanel No. 5 worn by women. But the smell of charas was even more provocative. He felt as though fire was flowing through every hair on his body.

'Suppose someone sees you?'

Suja spoke as though to herself when the smell of charas rose. She looked around. There was no one around. There were people on the road below them. Suppose Arora or someone else came up suddenly. Smoking in Haridwar was not just a crime, but a sin too, wasn't it?

'Don't, Ramesh, don't smoke.'

'Why did you fill it for me then?'

'I'm feeling scared.'

'That I'll have to go to jail? You idiot, do you know how many of these sanyasis are sitting on the banks of the Ganga and smoking opium. Only law has forbidden intoxicants in Haridwar. God has not forbidden it. I'm on god's side.'

Suja went back inside, sat on the chair and started reading

again. She looked up every now and then and glanced at Ramesh with restless eyes. He was inhaling deeply and had his gaze fixed on the street below. There were more people on the street now. The sun was going down. The number of beggars had increased under the trees. The wandering rickshaw-pullers, the carthorses that panted here and there, buildings that were dark even in daylight…

Was this Haridwar? Manasa Devi, is this your kingdom?

Ramesh's eyes shut slowly. The pipe which had gone out fell from between his clenched teeth.

Six

At 8 o'clock, Arora knocked on the door and entered the room. He brought the smell of some familiar perfume with him.

'Dinner, sir?'

'We'll eat here.'

'Sure, sir.'

He withdrew respectfully. Ramesh might have been Daksheswar and Suja Satidevi from the respect that Arora exhibited.

Ramesh was still sitting on the cane chair in the veranda. The pipe was clenched between his teeth. The white smoke of charas was still rising slowly from it. Suja continued to read.

Arora came back, bringing the menu. Suja looked through it. It did not have the chicken steak or the asparagus soup that she liked. Instead there was nan and peas korma and puri with curry.

'Nan and chicken korma,' Suja told Arora. She then called out to Ramesh in the veranda, 'What do you want, Ramesh?'

'I don't want anything.'

'Aren't you hungry?'

'No.'

'But you can't stay without eating anything.'

She got up and went and stood near him. Now, she was not his lover or his fiancée. She was his mother.

'I don't want anything.'

'Not even a sandwich?'

'I told you I don't want anything.' His voice was harsh.

He was a stubborn child now. Suja sighed and returned the menu card. When Arora took it and went away, she went back to her chair and picked up the book. But she did not read after that.

The waiter brought the food. He placed the plates and food on the small table and pushed it before Suja.

'Ramesh.'

She called out once more. He did not reply. He was sitting with his back to her, feet on the railing of the veranda.He was still smoking.

Suja spread the napkin on her lap and started eating. She was very hungry. She never gave up food when she was hungry. But Ramesh was used to starving. Eating was one of the things he hated the most.

After she finished her meal, Suja rubbed a little eau de cologne on her hands and went to the veranda.

'Ramesh.'

'Umm?'

'What do you mean by sitting like this?'

'Umm?'

'You have managed to destroy one evening completely, Ramesh!'

They had just three days. They had already lost one valuable evening. If he planned only to sit and smoke charas, he could have done that in Delhi as well. Why did they have to come to Haridwar for that?

'We have two more days.'

'Get up. Let's go for a walk somewhere.'

'Umm.'

But he did not get up from the chair. His voice was hoarse when he spoke. His hands trembled when he removed the pipe from his lips. Too much charas could make your voice break and your hands tremble.

The waiter came and removed the dishes. Suja could not finish everything. There was plenty of korma left in the porcelain dish. The waiter had brought apples for dessert. Suja cut one apple and held out a piece to Ramesh.

'Eat this at least.'

'You know I don't like sweet things.'

'Just a piece?' She pleaded.

He acted as though he had not heard and started preparing another pipe. Suja stood near him for a while. He did not speak at all. She stood looking at the street. Far away, at the temple of Manasa Devi, the lamps were burning. The street was emptying now. Darkness and light intermingled. The rickshaw-pullers were returning to their huts with empty vehicles. A day was ending.

Suja went back to her chair and opened her book again. She read till 10 o'clock. Arora came and asked if they needed anything.

'Water,' Ramesh muttered.

'I'll send it, sir. Good night.'

Arora went away. The waiter brought a jar of water covered with a lace doily and went away.

'Ramesh, aren't you coming in?'

Suja shut her book and sat looking at Ramesh. It was rarely that they got a chance to spend a night together. Each moment was valuable. But did he have any such thought? He'd been sitting like that for the last five or six hours. He didn't seem to be aware that he had someone with him.

Suja yawned as she got up from the chair. The double bed was covered with a white sheet. Near the head of the bed was a pedestal lamp with a batik shade. One could switch it on and off from the bed. Suja lay in the bed without changing her clothes. Her hair spread over the green sari.

'Ramesh!' she called once more. She felt lonely in the big bed. He did not respond to her call, but sat with his eyes fixed on the tip of the pipe clenched between his teeth. His eyes seemed to have lost the power of movement.

He would not come. There was no point calling him again. When she realised that, she turned towards the wall and lay on her side. She shut her eyes and lay like a fish, her back towards him. As she lay on her side, her shapely waist looked even more attractive...

Ramesh did not pay her any attention. His glance was fixed on the tip of the pipe as though it had been nailed there. After a while the pipe that was dead by now fell from his lips. His eyes closed by themselves.

After some time, he opened his eyes. His trembling fingers searched in his pocket and found another small bundle. He had already finished more than half of what he had brought from Delhi. He had smoked what would have been sufficient for five or six people all on his own.

He did not bother to heat it or powder it this time. He

did not add tobacco either. He opened the bundle and stuffed the whole thing into the pipe. His fingers trembled uncontrollably when he lit the match. He needed to strike a dozen matchsticks before he could get it going. He did not even know that he had burnt the index finger of his right hand and there was a blister there. It was not just the finger that burned – the whole of his body was burning.

When the smoke from the raw charas unmixed with tobacco reached his trachea, his eyes bulged out. His head and nose were burning, and his throat and mouth held the dryness of a whole desert.

After a while, that pipe too fell from his mouth.

He did not know how long he sat like that. Finally he got up slowly from the chair. It was difficult to stand on his weak legs. He put out the light and shut the door to the veranda. In the light that came through the batik shade he could see Suja sleeping on her side – without getting out of her sari, without tying her hair.

Two keys hung from the keyhole. He separated one from the ring. When he switched off the light, Suja disappeared in the darkness. There was only the sound of her breathing in the room.

He got out and locked the room from outside. All the rooms were dark. Everyone must be asleep. He went down the stairs slowly, holding on to the railing. It was dark downstairs too. Where was the light switch?

He stumbled out into the street. The crowds and noise of the day had vanished. The street was empty. Two or three rickshaws stood at the side of the road, looking abandoned. Beggars slept bent and curled up under the trees. He started walking through the Upar Sadak with his eyes open under the dim light of the street lamps – without knowing where he was going, why he was going. On hearing the sound of his footsteps in the silence, some birds that were still awake on the tree tops made a noise.

The Upar Sadak lay stretched out before and behind Ramesh. It would end at Har Ki Pauri in front of him and at Gadi Adda behind him. Once past the railway station, the Upar Sadak would change its name and go on to Jwalapur, from there to Rishikul and then to Gurukul. Behind him were the police station, the post office and the Lalta Rao Bridge. He knew what lay behind him. But what lay ahead of him?

His legs would not support him. His eyes were shutting every now and then. The fire of the charas still burned his senses. But he continued to walk. From the past to the future. From birth to death. From the womb to the pyre.

A beggar woman who was still awake, lying on the veranda of a shop hunted out her bowl in the dark and held it out towards Ramesh. 'Babuji, ek paisa.'

All she wanted was one paisa. Just one paisa. Were the pockets of his trousers fathoms deep? He pulled out a few coins and put them in her begging bowl. It took him a few minutes to find the coins in his pocket.

As he moved through the deserted street like a lost soul, he heard voices from behind him.

'Babuji, ek paisa.'

'Maharaj!'

'Beta!'

A number of begging bowls came towards him.

'Chup! Quiet!' He held his index finger to his lips and said.

His fathom-long hands went down into the pockets. When coins fell into the begging bowls, the beggars called on the gods to bless him.

The moon had come up by now. The shadows of the buildings that stood in rows on either side fell across the street. He pushed his tired hands into his pockets and continued his journey. As the only living shadow among the dead shadows. When he got tired of walking on the long street, he thought of changing his path.

There were galis, the usual narrow lanes, on either side of the street. They were just cracks between the row of buildings. He turned into the next gali he saw. It was on the right side of the street. A path that was very narrow and dark. On either side were the windowless walls of the greying buildings. The streets were stinking horribly of urine and other things. The moonlight did not reach the dark gali that did not have any lights at all. It was so dark.

He stumbled through the dark. He caught his foot against something.

'Ghrumm!' Someone got up with a grunt. He opened his eyes and looked. He could not see anything clearly. But he felt that something was moving in the dark. Was it just a feeling? Did the darkness breathe? There was the sound of panting breaths. Did the dark have life here? Did it have a shape and a nature?

He walked forward, dragging his feet with an effort. Someone was following him. There were footsteps just behind him. Daksha Prajapati, is it you? Dattatreya, is it you? Or, is it you, Bhageeratha? I'm seeking you. I did not see any of you at the railway station, there were only film stars. On the Upar

Sadak there were only the touts of hotels and the rickshaw-pullers. Were you hiding in this dark gali while I was looking for you?

He could see light at the end of the gali, perhaps a street lamp. He walked towards the light. The footsteps that followed him became quicker.

When he was almost at the light in the Lower Sadak, someone touched his shoulder. He turned back and looked and shook in fear.

'Who are you?'

The creature was clad in a black gown that covered it from head to toe. Its loose hair lay up to its chest. Its bloody tongue was thrust out of its mouth. There was a raised trident in its hand…

The creature did not reply but came forward and stood before Ramesh. He saw that it had a skull on a string round its neck.

'What do you want?'

The creature silently extended its hand. Ramesh moved back a step. Why did it hold out its hand? Did it want his blood? He leaned against the lamp post and asked once more, 'What do you want?'

There was no reply. The extended hand stayed there. Was it asking for money? Rather doubtfully, he took out a rupee from his pocket and put it on the extended palm. The creature took some flower petals from the skull around its neck and threw them towards him.

The chudail, or witch, did not stay there after that. It lifted the trident and went back into the dark gali. The darkness might be its place of residence. Though the creature itself had vanished from his sight, the long tongue, the skull on its chest and the trident did not vanish from Ramesh's mind. He did not believe in ghosts and ghouls. This was not death or even a kapalika, a member of that particular sect of Shaivism. Would a ghost ask for money? Only man needed money. So, that creature was a human being and nothing else.

He thought of going back into the lane and looking for the creature. He had seen one of the faces of Haridwar. Haridwar contained not just posters of film stars and rickshaws!

Ramesh continued his journey.

The Lower Sadak was narrower than the Upar Sadak. There were shops on either side that were linked together in a chain. Displays of costume jewellery glittered in the light of the street lamps. As he moved forward, the deserted Lower Sadak became narrower. It was now only as broad as a gali.

He could see something white in the middle of the road. A white shadow lay across the road, motionless. Was it another creature like the last one? A white one this time?

As he went closer, the size of the shadow increased. It was blocking the street, lying across it. He rubbed his eyes again and again and looked. His eyes could not see properly. His brain was not steady, he could not think. He was burning in the flame of the charas. Had he actually seen a creature like that? Weren't the long red tongue, the loose hair and the trident just the imagination of a weakened mind? Was this white shadow that lay across his way too just the creation of the charas?

What did it matter? Dreams and reality were all the same to him.

He walked forward a little way. He moved to the side of

the street, next to the veranda of a shop and rubbed his eyes once more to look more carefully. The shadow did not move, it did not make any sound. When he looked carefully, it looked as though the shadow were breathing. The huge white body was rising and falling. He gathered his courage and walked forward.

The white form became clearer. It had the shape of an animal. The body rose and fell in waves. He went closer and bent his head to take a better look. The creature had horns. And a tail. He extended his hand and touched it. It had soft hair on it. He rubbed its back and stomach gently.

When the cow moved, the bell around its neck sounded. The cow got to its knees, then got up and looked at him. Was it Nandini? Or Kamadhenu?

He looked, and then continued on his journey. He was sweating. The breeze that blew across the Ganga, beyond the buildings did not reach here. The lane was filled with heat and stench. He entered another lane that turned right from Lower Sadak. There were walls on either side, grey walls. Water lay stagnant on the ground. He could hear the drip of water somewhere.

He entered another gali from this one. He traversed the intertwined galis one by one. When he reached Bhalla Road, he heard the sound of a bell. The white cow came out of a gali nearby. When the cow saw him, it lifted its head slowly and raised its ears. Cow, are you also unable to sleep like me? Are you also a lost soul like me?

After half an hour, he found the white cow again. It was standing near Birla Road, leaning against a wall, listening for something. As though it were waiting for something.

When he got tired of walking and started to pant, Ramesh sat on the veranda of a shop. When his panting subsided, he entered the galis again. He did not know which lane he was walking through. One lane opened into another. That went on to join another. The galis joined together and separated again and again. Were they the paths of hell?

Where was his hotel? If he could reach the Upar Sadak, he could find the hotel. But where was Upar Sadak? Ramesh, who did not know the geography of Haridwar, wandered through the paths of hell. He could not walk a step further. Not just walk, he could not even sit. He needed to lay down his head and sleep. But where?

His tired legs brought him to sabjimandi, the vegetable market, again. He saw again, the chudail standing under a street lamp, trident in hand. The eyes looked like embers in the dimlight. The tips of the trident glinted…

'In which direction is the Upar Sadak?'

He walked through the path pointed to by the creature. The gali ended in Upar Sadak. He entered the street and staggered up to the hotel.

A cool breeze blew through the Upar Sadak. A cock crowed somewhere. The sky was turning pale beyond Manasa Devi's hill.

He hung on to the hand rail and tried to climb the steps upstairs. He couldn't. He thought he was going to fall. He somehow climbed them one at a time and reached upstairs. As he stood and panted, someone turned on the light.

'Where were you?'

Arora stood there, wearing just a towel and rubbing oil on his body. He looked at Ramesh with a stunned gaze. This was not the Ramesh he had seen the previous evening. Ramesh's cheeks had become shrunken, his eyes had developed deep shadows in one night. His slippers and trousers were covered with water and dirt.

'What happened? Tell me.'

Arora was really upset. Ramesh could not reply. His tongue would not move. He had managed to use up enough charas to intoxicate at least five people in one go. It was about twenty-four hours since he had had anything to eat. He had not slept the whole night. How many miles had he walked in the night? Why had he done all this? Why had he taken birth at all? Why was he living?

'Don't go out and wander alone in the night. This place is full of thieves and robbers. You have to be careful!' Arora continued to talk.

Ramesh took out the key from his pocket and opened the door. There was light in the room. Suja sat like a statue on the bed. The dampness in her eyes glinted in the dim light of the morning.

She covered her face with her hands and started sobbing.

Seven

Haridwar woke up.

The mist above Manasa Devi's hill had thinned and was spreading all over. Sunlight filled the valley. The green of the trees melted into the sunlight. The air held the faint perfume of the wicks wet with ghee that had been lighted the previous evening. Suja stood near the window, looking at the morning in Haridwar.

Ramesh was lying motionless on the bed. He was sleeping the sleep of the dead. She had removed his dirty clothes even as he slept and covered him with a sheet. Her eyes filled with tears every time she looked at him. He looked as though he had the ague.

She took a bath and wore fresh clothes. Avinash Arora had brought some jasmine flowers she did not know from where.

'You may like these,' he had held them out and smiled.

She wore a cotton sari, wore the flowers in her wet hair and waited for Ramesh to wake up. It was ten o'clock when he finally woke up.

'Ramesh, how are you now? How do you feel?'

She went and sat near him when she saw that he had opened his eyes. He sat for a while with his face buried in his hands. He felt as though his head was made of granite. It was so heavy!

'Go take a bath. You'll feel better after a bath,' she said.

He got up like an obedient child and walked to the bathroom. My dear girl, forgive me. I have made you cry in Haridwar too. I've made you cry so many times! Please forgive me!

He stood under the shower and let the cold water flow over him like rain. He felt as though the pain in his body was being squeezed out by the water. When he came out of the bathroom, he was still tired, but felt pleased with life.

'Aren't you hungry? It's so long since you ate anything!'

'I could eat an elephant.'

He laughed. Laughter had returned to his face. After a deep sleep for four hours, a bath and a fresh set of clothes, he was a new man. There was light in the sunken eyes.

They sat on either side of the table on the ground floor of the hotel. Food and glasses and plates and cutlery were spread on the table.

'Is it the elephant or the rhinoceros that is heavier?' Suja asked as she spooned porridge into her mouth.

'The rhino.'

'No,' she argued. 'The elephant is heavier.'

'The rhino is heavier.'

'The elephant is.'

'The rhino is not as big as the elephant, but it is heavier and stronger.'

'The elephant weighs more and is stronger.'

'What's going on here?' Arora came in and heard them arguing.

'It's the rhino.'

'It's the elephant. Mr Arora, tell us. Which is stronger and heavier, the elephant or the rhinoceros?' Suja turned towards Arora.

Arora was well dressed as always. He wore a white shirt with a red tie. He stood there confused by her question. Actually, he did not know whether the elephant was heavier or the rhinoceros.

'Mr Arora, your reply should be impartial.'

As he opened his mouth to say something, Suja remembered that Arora, being a man, might take sides with a man.

Arora thought for a while, then delivered the judgement, 'The elephant is heavier, but the rhinoceros is stronger.'

'You are very diplomatic, Mr Arora!' Suja said as she moved the porridge bowl away.

'Please call me Avinash, Mrs Ramesh,' he requested her.

'But, what's your name, Avinash?'

Hearing that, Avinash Arora laughed aloud.

'Why aren't you laughing, Suja?'

'That's not a joke, it's a cliché.'

'Ho, ho, ho,' Avinash continued to laugh.

Suja said, 'Liar.'

'Am I?'

He went away, smiling at Suja. Suja poured out the tea into two cups. As usual, she put one cube of sugar in Ramesh's cup and three in her own. Ramesh did not like anything sweet.

'I'm a narcotic addict.' This was the reason Ramesh gave for his dislike of sweet things.

'I'm not a narcotic addict.' Suja also had to have a reason for liking sweet things.

'What's the programme today?'

As they finished eating and climbed the stairs, Avinash appeared. He said, 'If it's convenient for you, you could come to my house.'

'We're planning to visit Manasa Devi, Avinash,' Suja told him.

They were planning to climb Manasa Devi's hill in the morning. Ramesh was not very keen on it. How would he have the strength to climb mountains?

'Where are you from?' asked Ramesh.

'Jwalapur.'

Jwalapur isn't very far from Haridwar. You could call it a part of Haridwar if you liked.

'Who's there at home, Avinash?' It was Suja who asked.

'My father, mother, grandfather, my wife, three children, my younger sister, servants, buffaloes, cows, a dog... I have a big family.'

'Only a dog? Don't you have cats?' she asked.

'No, there are no cats,' he shook his head.

'Don't you like cats?'

'Cats steal.'

'And dogs?'

'No, our dog is not a thief.'

'If so, your cat would also not steal.'

'But Avinash does not have a cat, Suja,' Ramesh intervened.

Avinash came up with them. He started talking about Delhi. He had gone to the city a number of times. He liked Delhi much better than Haridwar. Delhi had shagufas and discotheques. There were hotels with floor shows and strip teases.

'There's nothing in Haridwar. It is such a bore. I'm fed up with Haridwar.'

If he had had a choice he would have escaped from this accursed Haridwar. He would have sought shelter in some big city – a city which had shagufas and discotheques.

'We are fed up with the city,' Ramesh and Suja said. Avinash found that surprising.

'We're looking for an escape from Delhi.'

'I don't believe you.'

'You're a citomaniac, Avinash. We, on the other hand, are citophobiacs.'

'Did you understand what Suja said, Avinash?'

'Avinash, are you a kissophobe or a kissophile?'

Avinash struggled to understand.

Ramesh said, 'I'm a kissophone.'

'Kissophone…?'

Suja's laughter scattered in the room.

'Why do you laugh? Isn't kissing a language? Kissing is a language like Malayalam or English. Ants are kissophones. They communicate through kissing. Suja, have you noticed the behaviour of ants?'

Avinash looked at Ramesh and Suja, in turn. He then asked, 'So, when will you both come to Jwalapur?'

'Whenever you like.'

'Tonight?' Avinash asked eagerly.

'Agreed,' Ramesh said.

'Agreed,' Suja too said.

'So, dinner at Jwalapur tonight.' Avinash was effervescent with happiness. He whistled and took the stairs down three steps at a time. After a while, he came back upstairs.

'If you wish to see Manasa Devi, it would be better for you to go before the sun is high. You won't be able to climb the hill when the day is advanced.'

He walked up and down the room. The temple of Manasa Devi was right on top of the hill. The pilgrims who wanted to go to the temple went up and came down the hill before noon.

'We are just going. Thank you, Avinash.'

Since they had to walk up the hill, Suja wore a churidar and kurta instead of a sari. Ramesh had painted the kurta himself – his gift on her last birthday.

'Is it easy to do batik?' Avinash asked interestedly. Everyone in Delhi was crazy about batik. Batik saris and kurtas were all the rage in colleges and at dinners and functions.

'You just need to know a little chemistry. The process is easy.'

'What is difficult?'

'To paint the design. You have to be creative.'

Ramesh and Suja got out of the hotel. The sunlight melted and flowed. Silver serpents moved on the tarred road. The horses pulling tongas through Upar Sadak that radiated heat were panting.

'Saptadhara, four rupees.'

'Khangal, three rupees.'

The tongawalas and the rickshaw-pullers were yelling out. Disappointing all of them, Ramesh and Suja walked through Upar Sadak.

'Babuji!...Memsaab!...'

One rickshaw-puller, a young man in a lungi, wearing a tiger claw pendant around his neck, was not willing to let them go.

'Nahi chahiye! We don't want a rickshaw!'

He pedalled after them, not paying any attention to what Ramesh said.

'Babuji!... Memsaab!...' he continued to recite like an incantation. He was very young and seemed as strong as a horse. He followed Ramesh and Suja for about a furlong.

'Will you take us where we want to go?'

'Yes, Babuji!' The rickshaw-puller jumped down from his seat and bowed before Ramesh with folded hands. He bowed to Suja too. He then wiped the seat of the rickshaw.

'You need give me only what you want to, Babuji!'

'Climb up, Suja.'

'Ramesh!' Suja continued to hesitate. Ramesh got into the rickshaw and then helped her up.

'Where do you want to go, Babuji?'

Ramesh pointed to the top of the hill of Manasa Devi.

'That's where we're going.'

'Babuji!'

'You said you'd take us wherever we wanted.'

The rickshaw-puller swallowed hard. He seemed to be about to break into tears. Ramesh and Suja got down from the rickshaw. Ramesh took out a rupee note from his pocket and asked, 'What's your name?'

'Hanuman.'

Suja laughed when she heard the name. Hanuman was reluctant to take the money.

'Take it, Hanuman,' Suja spoke persuasively.

Hanuman took the money.

'Are you from this place?'

'From Sholapur.'

Hanuman folded his hands, turning to Ramesh and Suja in turn and withdrew.

'That was very naughty of you,' Suja chided Ramesh when Hanuman had gone. And then she started laughing loudly.

They turned from Upar Sadak to the path that led to the hill of Manasa Devi. The steps started from the road itself. After some steps there was a path that was even. Then came steps and then a path again. Steps again…Hawkers sat on either side of the steps. A young girl stood with a basket full of flowers. There were sellers of coconuts, puffed rice and sandal sticks. There were sellers of groundnuts. The flowers and incense sticks were for Manasa Devi. The groundnuts were for the monkeys.

'Flowers for Manasa Devi…'

'Coconuts for Manasa Devi…'

The hawkers shouted from either side. There was a leper among them. He was filling leaf containers with petals that he plucked with his deformed fingers.

'A good leper. He's not begging,' Suja stated.

The devotees were buying flowers form the leper as well. There was no deformity and disease here. There was only devotion. They bought flowers for the goddess from him.

'Beta!' Someone called at the starting point of the steps. Ramesh turned around and looked. It was an old woman. She came with a leaf container full of flowers.

'Give this to the goddess, son. I can't climb the hill.' She held out the container.

The old woman turned towards the temple on the hill that she could no longer climb and folded her hands. She murmured something. Her voice trembled and her eyes filled with tears. After a little while, she wiped her eyes and walked away. Ramesh stood and looked as she walked, hunched almost double. She had some deep sorrow. Sorrow at this age even…

Ramesh and Suja started climbing the steps.

'Ramesh, what shall we pray to the goddess for?'

'Peace of mind.'

He did not wish for wealth or a long life. All he wanted was some peace. That was all he wanted.

'Fifty, fifty-one, fifty-two…,' Suja kept counting as they went up the steps. Manasa Devi, we are coming, with flowers and incense, we are coming to you.

There were devotees behind them too. There were people from villages and people from cities. There were old people and children. People who had lost their limbs, people who were ill…With offerings in their hands and prayers on their lips they were climbing the hill.

The pilgrims who had set out very early in the morning were coming down the hill in groups. There were beggars on either side of the path. There were people with terrible diseases and people who were so old that they were nearly half dead. Ramesh and Suja climbed the hill, putting coins into the begging bowls on either side.

Processions of devotees went up and down the hill. Ramesh and Suja joined them, unknown among the crowd.

'Look at that!' Suja pointed out. There was a red tree near the temple. A tree that was the colour of blood. The trunk and the smaller branches were all red. Was there a mention of a red tree somewhere in botany?

Manasa Devi's hill was under a blanket of green. There

were trees and bushes all over. That red tree stood apart among the canopy of green. As soon as they reached the top he would look at that tree. He would pluck the red leaves. If possible he would break some twigs and bring them down.

The first peculiar sight he had seen in Haridwar was that creature with the trident. The second peculiar sight was this red tree.

Suja had not seen the creature. He would find it and show it to Suja. It would be wandering in one of the lanes that separated into many strands, with the long red tongue hanging out of its mouth, trident in hand, skull hanging from its neck.

'One hundred and eighteen, one hundred and nineteen, one hundred and twenty...'

Suja continued to count the steps. Would she be able to count all the steps spread before them without making a mistake? Others were coming up the steps they had already traversed. Haridwar was growing smaller down below. One could see the roofs of buildings spreading on all sides.

'Two hundred.'

Suja sat on one of the steps, panting. She kept the leaf containers on her lap and said, 'I can't do it.'

Ramesh was a few steps behind her. He also stopped when he reached her. He massaged her back that was rising and falling with her panting. His hands stumbled over the bra under the kurta.

Manasa Devi's temple was up there somewhere. There were so many steps to climb still! There was such a distance to cover!

'Get up!'

Ramesh pulled her up by her hand. She collected the flower packets and started climbing again.

'Two hundred and one, two hundred and two, two hundred and three . . .'

People kept passing them. She thought they should not sit anywhere again. They would rest in the presence of the goddess.

The Ganga lay like a ribbon beyond the roofs. Far away, were the saptadharas, the seven tributaries.

The steps ended. From then on, there was only a narrow path between trees and groups of rocks. A man was selling thick red thread where the steps ended. Ramesh and Suja bought a roll of thread each.

Hermits had built huts under the trees and lived there. Some of them sat behind a picture of the Devi and asked for alms. They could hear someone reciting Sanskrit slokas from up somewhere.

When the hermits who went up and down the hill met, they greeted each other with, 'Jai Sankar!'

Monkeys were playing on the branches of the trees. They would come down from the tree when they saw people. Suja sat on a rock and fed the monkeys groundnuts. They started dancing around her on their hind legs. She picked up a small monkey and put it on her lap.

'A rehearsal?'

'Don't be impudent!' Suja's face was red. She held the baby monkey close and started humming the lines of some lullaby.

As they continued upwards, the Sanskrit stanzas became clearer.

Maam cha yovyabhicharena…
(Serving me with unswerving devotion…)

They saw an aged hermit sitting under thick creepers that looked like serpents tangled together. His hair was matted. The thin twig-like body was covered only by a breechclout. He held an old book in his trembling hands.

Brahmano hi pratishtaham
Amritasyavyayasya cha
Saswatasya cha dharmasya
Sukhasyaikantikasya cha.
(I am the abode of brahman, immortal and immutable, of dharma that is everlasting and of bliss that is absolute.)

Though the voice was trembling, it was tuneful. People put money on the saffron cloth spread before him and walked on. Ramesh and Suja sat on a low rock before the hermit. He did not pay them any attention. He sat as though his mission in life was nothing but to read out Sanskrit stanzas from this old book. Stanzas flowed in a trembling voice from the dry throat:

Na tat bhasyatesuryo
Na sasanko na pavaka
Yatgatwananivartante
Taddhama paramam mama.
(The sun does not shine there,
nor the moon, nor fire;
to which having gone, they do not return.
That is my supreme abode.)

When he had finished reciting Purushothamayogam, they got up. They had a long way to go still. As they walked up the narrow path, they saw footprints on the rock. The thousands of pilgrims who came every day had left their mark on the rock…

They finally reached the temple of Manasa Devi, faces burnt dark by the sun, drenched in sweat. As he climbed the last few steps, Ramesh was panting like an old, run-down horse. All around them were devotees exhausted by the steep climb. The monkeys crowded around, creating a racket to get groundnuts.

They went and stood before the temple, flowers and incense in hand. Manasa Devi, we have come. Traversing cities and villages, crossing rivers, climbing hills, here we stand before your sacred presence. Show us the way… Beyond the burning lamps, Manasa Devi stood, a constant smile in her merciful eyes. The sacrificial fire was burning. They placed the flowers at the feet of the goddess and the incense and other perfumes in the sacrificial fire. The bells of the temple were ringing. They too went around the temple following the others, two anonymous shadows in the flow of pilgrims.

Ramesh did not think about Delhi. He forgot his mother who lived only for him and the girl who accompanied him like a shadow. In that moment when he forgot even himself, his mind caught the flames of the sacrificial fire and rang with the bells of the temple. He felt his legs growing weak.

'Look!'

Her voice woke him from the frozen state in which he had lost even his existence, in which he had drowned in the sacrificial fire and the ringing of the bells.

'Umm?' he asked with a start.

'Look at that!'

He now recognized the girl who walked close to him. He looked in the direction in which she was pointing. The red tree.

They went down the steps darkened with burnt oil and walked towards the tree. The red tree that they had looked at with such wonder from down below was right before them. But it was just an ordinary tree. It was green like any other tree. The red threads that the devotees had tied year after year had given it a red halo. It was a tree that was clad in red threads from top to bottom, on its trunk and its branches.

There was an idol of the goddess under the tree. There were red threads around the idol too; they were slick with oil.

Ramesh took out the red threads they had bought at the hillside. They moved towards the tree with the threads in their hands.

'What shall we pray for?' Ramesh asked. One had to make a wish as one tied the thread around the tree. The belief was that the goddess would grant that wish. 'What shall we wish for, Suja?'

She stood there, head bent, without saying anything in reply. She would have to decide what to ask the goddess for. What should it be? Would it be that she should get a first class in her examinations? Or, that the piles that troubled her father constantly should become better?

'Have you thought of a wish?'

She was silent and stood with her head bent. Her face held an expression that was strange to him. Those eyes that held the beauty of a peacock feather fluttered. There was the rose tint of shyness around her lips.

What could he pray for? He thought for a moment. My

mother who lives alone, far away. My mother who lives only for me. Who could he pray for, but for that mother?

'I've decided to pray for my mother.'

She continued to be silent.

She stood under the tree with the red thread in her hands. As she tied it to one of the lower branches of the tree, her eyes shut by themselves and her lips murmured something.

'What did you pray for?'

She just bent her head without replying.

He put his hand on her shoulder and insisted, 'Tell me. Was it for your father?'

She shook her head.

'To get a first class in your examinations?'

'No.'

'Then what?'

She lifted her head and looked at him with kohl-darkened eyes that were like burning lamps.

'I've got it. Stupid girl!'

She continued to stand with her head bent, but laughed silently.

Ramesh stood with the red thread in his hands and hesitated. There were many prayers that he wanted to make. How could he ask the goddess to grant all of them? He had to choose one. He could pray for his mother or for Suja…

'Quickly, Ramesh,' Suja reminded him. People kept coming and tying threads and going away. They came with a prayer on their lips and tied the thread. The branches of the tree were bending under the weight of the threads.

'Oh goddess! Please end the blood baths in Vietnam and Biafra!' Ramesh tied his thread.

They came down slowly, walking over the roots that spread all over the narrow path, and the rocks that were scattered all over. Manasa Devi, give us leave to depart. I'll come to you again at least once. If not in this birth, in the next one. If not as a man, as an animal. I'll come.

Dhyayato vishayan pumsa
Sangasteshupajayate
Sangatat sanjayate kama
Kamat krodhobhijayate
(A man thinks of objects and gets attached to them.
From attachment desire is born and from desire comes anger.)

The hermit sat below and continued to read. His throat seemed hoarse from reciting continuously. The recitation seemed to have become a sad cry.

'What's the meaning of the stanza that he's just finished reciting?' Suja asked as she went down the steep path, holding on to his hand.

The meaning of that stanza, young girl? The stanza that has been at the tip of my tongue for so many years. Those stanzas that my mother explained to me years and years back.

But he said, 'I don't know.'

It's better that you do not know.

Eight

Some train passed, blowing its whistle through the valley by the hill of Manasa Devi. The birds that had been resting on the branches of trees rose in a formation. The flapping of wings rang in their ears. Ramesh, who was lying down on the untrodden grass among the bushes, opened his eyes.

'Suja!'

'Umm?'

'Some train.'

'Umm.'

She sat up on the grass. Her face was sweaty and her hair had come loose. Her neck and hair held the smell of his aftershave. His chest smelled of the shampoo she used.

'Will Manasa Devi forgive us?'

'We didn't do anything that would displease the goddess, Suja.'

She got up with a smile and went and sat a little away in a hermitage that had been built by nature with creepers and branches of trees. She started combing her hair.

'Dhyayato vishayan pumsa'

(Man thinks of objects…)

Ramesh lay flat on his back and sent up the cigarette smoke. He laughed to himself.

'I'm thinking of Delhi.'

Though the train had passed, its roar lingered in the valley. A train that had come from Mussoorie or Dehradun, on its way to Delhi. It awoke his memories of the city.

'Ramesh!'

'Umm?'

'Do you like Haridwar or Delhi better?' She called out, sitting at a distance from him.

It was difficult to answer. Sometimes he felt very fond of Delhi, and at other times, he hated the city. They had just come to Haridwar. So, he had not started hating it yet. If he stayed two full days here, he might start hating Haridwar too. He sent cigarette smoke spiralling up and wondered: is there anything I like permanently in this world? Sometimes when he thought of his mother, he felt choked with the love he felt. At other times, thoughts of her brought no feeling at all. His mind would just feel frozen. Suja? When he thought of her tomorrow, he might have the same frozen feeling in his mind. I don't know myself. He lay on his stomach on the grass and looked at her. But at this moment, I love you. You are the human creature I love the most on this earth.

What have I gained in this life? He kept his face close to the blue smoke that had been imprisoned in the green grass. What was it? Was it the job with Hirozi that paid him a four-figure salary? The car that he was going to buy? The tour he had made the previous winter through Latin America? His mother's love?

'Ramesh, what are you thinking about?'

He answered without lifting his face from the cigarette smoke that lay crushed in the green grass, 'About you.'

'About me?'

'Umm. You are the one valuable thing I possess in this life.'

She got up from her hermitage and came running towards him. Her eyes had opened more than they could really open. She pressed her face where the sweat was drying out, on the back of his neck. No, I have not achieved anything in my life, he thought. I've only wished to achieve. It is an illusion to believe that I have achieved. But by the time he opened his mouth to say that, her face with its taste of salt covered his mouth.

'Ramesh, I love you!'

He knew that. She had said it a thousand times, proved it a thousand times. She got up from near him and went and stood a little apart under a tree and said, 'Ramesh, I love you!'

She went and sat in a thicket with flowers and vines and repeated, 'Ramesh, I love you!'

'Poor girl!' he spoke to himself.

He lay looking up at the sky and lit another cigarette. Above him the sky was a dark blue. As he lay there letting the smoke rise lazily, he could not help wishing: if only I were a part of this sky! If only I were a small drop in this blue ocean…

His eyes were closing again. After wandering here and there, speaking to the monkeys and the birds, she came back, knelt beside him and said, 'Ramesh, you are my life!'

When they started feeling hungry, they came out of the bushes and started walking through the narrow path towards the valley. On their way, they saw two small idols of Shiva and Parvati that stood touching each other. There was a soot-darkened mud lamp in front of the idols that were covered in turmeric and oil.

'Ramesh, these idols are you and me.'

She knelt before the idols. She put her hand on one of them hesitantly. The idols that are you and me. She then hugged them, with tenderness.

The hill did not seem to end though they went down and down. It was more difficult coming down than going up. If you slipped you could fall and hit your head or go rolling down right to the bottom. They came down the path that held the footprints of countless pilgrims. The roofs of Haridwar became clearer. Beyond the rooftops lay the Ganga, melting in the midday sun. The Saptadhara became clearer beyond the trees.

'One, two, three…,' Suja started counting as they came down the steps.

As they left the last step and came on to the path they heard a feeble voice, 'Children…'

It was the old woman they had seen on their way up. She came staggering towards them.

'Did you give the flowers to the goddess, children?'

'Yes, mother.'

She straightened her bent back a little and lifted her hand as though to bless Ramesh and Suja, 'May the goddess bless you, children.'

She stood for a moment, looking at the temple of Manasa Devi far away on top of the hill. Tears filled her sunken, greying eyes.

'Mother!'

'It's nothing, nothing...'

She wiped away the tears with her palm and started walking away unsteadily. Who was she? What was her sorrow? Ramesh and Suja stood and looked as she walked away slowly.

They reached the Upar Sadak again. The burning street where the sweat of horses and men fell, the weary rickshaw-pullers and the horses. They stood on the side of the street trying to decide where they should go next. There were so many places for them to see – Kusha Ghat, Neel Dhara, the hermitage of the seven sages or Saptarishi Ashram, Bhimgoda, Shravana Nath Temple, Anjana Devi Temple, Satidevi Temple, Daksha Mahadev Temple... They had not even seen the Brahma Kund.

They had just one and a half days to see everything. The Mussoorie Express would come and wait in Haridwar for them the next night. They had to see everything before that. Each moment was precious.

'Let's go see Bhimgoda,' Ramesh decided. Bhimgoda was just one mile away – on the Rishikesh Road. They decided that they would have something to eat and then go there.

As they crossed the road, they saw Hanuman.

'Babuji!'

Hanuman's teeth gleamed in a smile when he saw them. He slowed down his pedalling and came and stopped near them. A fat man was dozing in the heat of the midday sun in the rickshaw.

'Did you see the Deviji?' Hanuman started talking as though he had known them for a long time.

'Where are you going, Hanuman?'

'Up to the Gadi Adda, the railway station. What about you, Memsaab?'

'Will you take us to Bhimgoda?'

'Need you ask, Memsaab?' Hanuman was enthusiastic. The fat passenger was still fast asleep. Hanuman said that he would take him to the railway station and return immediately, and pedalled away.

They did not feel like going to the hotel. There were vendors who sold eatables on the roadside. Suja could feel her mouth watering when she saw the bhaturas being fried and smelt the spicy chana. The pot with the chana stood on a four-legged stand. Green chillies stood up in the pot. The bhaturas dripped oil in an aluminium vessel. A couple of rickshaw-pullers were squatting on their haunches and eating. One or two beggars too.

'Two plates, bhai.'

The bhatura seller looked at Ramesh and Suja in turn. One could see the disbelief in his eyes. Their appearance and dress did not seem to match people who ate stuff prepared in roadside carts. How could the bhatura seller in Haridwar know that they were used to eating rice and potato curry in bits of plantain leaf, standing in the midst of the teeming crowd at the Gadi Adda in Old Delhi, in the company of beggars and madmen?

They ate the bhatura and chana and waited for Hanuman. In less than five minutes, Hanuman came panting. The veins on his forehead were swollen, perhaps from the heat of the sun. Sweat poured down his chest with its tiger claws.

'Hanuman, have you eaten?'

'That doesn't matter, Memsaab.'

Hanuman showed no interest in food. He was so happy to have found Suja and Ramesh. He cleaned the seat of the rickshaw. The marks made by the weight of the fat merchant could still be seen.

Hanuman was reluctant to accept the bhatura and chana. But once he did, he ate them greedily. He might not have had anything that day. A glass of water on top of it filled Hanuman's belly. Streams of sweat flowed down his strong chest.

Hanuman, whose hunger had been satisfied, split the sunlight as he pedalled with renewed strength. The rickshaw moved along the street behind the Brahma Kund. If one looked from Har Ki Paudi, one could see the distant range of hills. The Ganga entered Haridwar, splitting the mountain into two. The rickshaw turned to the left. It moved up another side of Manasa Devi's hill. This was the path that led to Rishikesh and Badrinath and Kailas, this was the path that led to Vaikuntha, the path to heaven.

Hanuman stopped the rickshaw near Bhimgoda. Ramesh and Suja got down and Hanuman pushed the rickshaw to the side of the path.

'I'll wait here, Saab,' he said and lit a beedi.

Ramesh and Suja walked to Bhimgoda. The five Pandavas had walked this way on their road to heaven. When he thought that he was walking the path that had been trodden by Emperor Yudhishthira, Ramesh felt thrilled. He was walking over the footsteps of the Pandavas. How could his feet not feel the thrill?

On the sides of the hill, hermits had dug out caves and

made their abode there. They could see oil lamps burn in the caves where daylight did not enter. Ramesh and Suja stood near the pond. The water was clear and they could see the reflections of the temple that stood on the side of the pond and the hill beyond it.

They took off their slippers and sat on the steps leading down to the pond. There was water up to the fifth step from the top. The water was clear as crystal. It was sacred water, water created by Bhimasena, the second Pandava. As he sat looking at the water, the picture of Kurukshetra appeared before Ramesh's inner eye. He felt that the sound of Achyuta's conch, Panchajanya, could be heard somewhere far off.

Sannyasam karmanam Krishna
Punaryogam cha shamsasi
Yacchreya etayorekam
Tanme bruhi sunischitam
(Krishna, you preach renunciation and then again action.
Tell me certainly which of the two is better.)

The cry of Arjuna who was burning in intense sorrow came to Ramesh's ears from Kurukshetra. His eardrums trembled at the sound of the conches, Devadatta and Paundra.

The grandfather of the Kurus lay on his bed of arrows, covered with wounds.

Time was passing. All that had to be done on this earth had been done. The Pandavas reached Haridwar on their way to heaven. Haridwar was the boundary between heaven and earth. Bhimasena decided to build a memorial in Haridwar to show that he had passed this way. He knelt and pressed his knee to the earth and created this pond. The water from

Ganga that flowed at a distance travelled through the earth and filled this pond. Ramesh and Suja were now sitting near the pond that was created by Bhimasena's knee.

They went down the steps and sat on the fifth step. The steps were dirty with oil and fading flowers. The water was full of floating flowers. They took the water in their palms and drank it. The water held the taste of salt from Bhimasena's sweat.

'We are free from all sins from today.'

'But what sins have we committed, Ramesh?'

'The sin of living.'

Ramesh was feeling a terrible need to light a cigarette. Could he smoke here? In this sacred place? He who had sat and smoked charas in this sacred land was now hesitating to smoke a cigarette. He who had insulted the gods was now showing respect to the sons of Pandu who were human.

Some devotees came and stood on the other side of the pond. There were men, women and children among them. All of them immersed themselves in the water of the pond and bathed.

They went away with the satisfaction that they had washed away all their sins.

'Babuji!'

That was Hanuman's voice. He had got fed up of waiting for Ramesh and Suja and had come in search of them. They awoke at the sound of his voice – as though from a sleep that had lasted aeons.

'Shouldn't we go, Babuji?'

'We shall go, Hanuman.'

They got up from the step. Their clothes were soiled with

the oil and dirt. Ramesh's trousers and Suja's churidaar were wet up to the knees. They walked with Hanuman towards the rickshaw.

The hermits who lived in the dark caves, in the light of the burning lamps, renounced the world and remained immersed in meditation – their long, matted hair had the colour of the roots of the trees that grew on the sides of the caves. Aged limbs that sought to go back to the earth.

'Where do you want to go, Babuji?'

'Wherever you like, Hanuman.'

Hanuman showed his strong teeth and laughed.

'Upar Sadak, Babjuji?'

'Umm, all right.'

They had come from Upar Sadak, hadn't they? They would return there. Hanuman pedalled through the cooling sun, working his strong muscles. When they passed Har Ki Pauri and reached Upar Sadak, he slowed down.

'Babuji, have you seen the statue of Mrityunjaya?'

'No.'

'Shall I take you there?'

'If it's not too far.

They had no objection to going anywhere. They had come to see everything. They would see whatever they could.

The rickshaw went past the junction where Bhalla Road and Birla Road met. Hanuman took off his vest that was soaked in sweat and placed it on the step of the rickshaw. There were a thousand reflections of the sun on his back. The streets were alive now. There were people moving in groups. The horse carts and rickshaws struggled to move among them. There was not even one stylishly dressed person among them.

One could not spy a pair bell-bottomed of trousers or even a go-go kurta.

'Look Babuji, look Memsaab!' Hanuman pointed.

There was a big lotus carved out of stone. The petals opened out in the stone. Lord Mrityunjaya sat on the lotus. Around his neck were serpents that stuck out their tongues. He had four hands. Two of them held a deer and a string of rudraksha beads. The two hands raised above his head held the kamandalu, the spouted pot carried by sages, and water flowed from it endlessly on him. The water collected in the stone lotus.

Ramesh and Suja scooped up the water from the lotus and washed their faces.

Mrityunjaya, give us leave to go.

When they reached the hotel, Suja opened her handbag and held out a ten-rupee note to Hanuman.

'I don't have any change, Memsaab.'

'Never mind.' She made him take the note. Hanuman's hands trembled as though he had fever.

'Are you on a fast or something?' Avinash, who had been waiting for them, came out of the hotel.

'We had our fill of bhatura and chana.' Suja replied as she went up the stairs.

Avinash's forehead wrinkled at that.

'Don't invite dysentery,' he warned them with affection.

Ramesh entered the room, turned the fan on at full speed and fell on to the bed. Suja joined him.

Nine

'May I come in, please?' Avinash asked from beyond the door.

'Just a moment.'

Suja was putting on a sari and Ramesh was sitting on the floor, helping her with the pleats.

'Come in, please.'

Suja tucked in the pleats. Ramesh went and sat leaning back in his chair. Avinash, all dressed-up, came into the room. A terylene shirt and trousers. A tie as usual. Why was he wearing a tie in this terrible heat?

'Haven't you got ready yet?'

Ramesh had only put on his trousers. His naked chest showed the ribs clearly. From there, on either side, a line of hair came down to the navel. Avinash Arora had no hair on his face or limbs. His face had the smoothness of a girl's.

'Hurry up!' he tried to rush them.

Ramesh got up and washed his face at the washbasin. He sprayed his chest and underarms with eau de cologne.

'Is it imported?'

Avinash picked up the bottle of eau de cologne. He was following each of Ramesh's movements carefully. He seemed to have grown to like Ramesh's long body and the way he dressed and talked. He might even have become an admirer.

'You are very manly!' he had once said in the course of a conversation.

'Avinash, is your wife beautiful?' Suja asked as she put a bindi on her forehead.

'Not as beautiful as you.'

She was wearing a light blue chiffon sari. A light blue bindi that matched the sari was on her forehead and her eyes were lined with kohl. Avinash could not draw his eyes away from her face. Ramesh noticed that.

When Avinash went down to call a taxi, he said with a laugh, 'He has fallen for you.'

'The taxi is here,' Avinash's voice came from downstairs.

She picked up her handbag and Ramesh picked up his tobacco tin. They locked the door and went downstairs.

'Ladies first,' Avinash opened the door of the car for her. She sat between Avinash and Ramesh in the back seat. The car passed the idol of Mrityunjaya and went towards Jwalapur.

Sitting in the car, Avinash spoke about his life. He did not want to spend all his life running a hotel in Haridwar. He wanted to become an executive in a big city like Delhi or Bombay.

'There's life in places like Delhi. There's nothing here. Nothing at all.' His face looked as though he had swallowed something bitter as he said this.

'To be frank, I hate Haridwar.'

Did Haridwar have no life? Was Haridwar boring? Ramesh could not understand. Pilgrims from all over the country came here. People who spoke different languages! People of all castes and classes. People who came with such different experiences! How could he get bored with this Haridwar?

'There is nothing in big cities, Avinash. There is only an outward show, no life. There are only performances. We city dwellers are just actors.'

'I like acting.'

Avinash Arora was sitting with his eyes fixed on the speedometer of the car. Suddenly Ramesh felt that he could understand his feelings. Hadn't he also had the same thoughts as Avinash? When he was in the village, he would feel that he wanted to reach Delhi. When he was in Delhi, he would wish he could somehow go to the village. If this Avinash Arora had lived in Delhi, he would have said: I hate this Delhi, there's no life here.

Ramesh had started liking Haridwar from that morning. He preferred the hill of Manasa Devi where hermitages were scattered and you could hear the sound of the Vedas being chanted to the luxury of Asoka Hotel.

Ramesh and Avinash were polar opposites. And yet they had grown to like each other and could perhaps even become friends.

The car reached Jwalapur town. This was the commercial area of Haridwar. Lorries laden with sacks of wheat came and went.

Vast fields of wheat lay on either side. The rays of the setting sun fell on the fields. Her eyes felt as though they had been touched with snow. Suja felt like getting down from the car and running through the fields.

'Avinash, is your house next to wheat fields?'

'Umm.' He just grunted. He did not have any interest in

wheat fields. Suja was feeling jealous of him. He could wake up to the sight of these green fields. He could wander any time through these green sprouts. He could sleep at night fanned by winds bearing the smell of these fields.

'I don't come home every day. Only once a week.'

She felt bad when she heard Avinash say that. Avinash, you are cruel.

He had a scooter and could reach home in half an hour. And yet he would go home only once in a while. There were reasons, he explained. There was no bathtub at home. The food was not cooked in the western way. There wasn't even electricity.

There was a dry pond. There was also a board, termite eaten, standing on a pole, that said, 'No Entry'. The car stopped there. They had to walk the rest of the way. They walked through a lane. They could see the marks of wheels on the path. The marks made by the wheels of Avinash's scooter when he had came the previous week.

There were some plants with small leaves, growing wildly.

'What plant is this?' Suja enquired.

'Ban.'

Ban was a type of cotton that was used to make quilts, Avinash explained. Didn't Suja who was a Punjabi know that? The ban plants had not yet flowered. Ramesh walked through the ban plants, a Philip Morris between his lips. Before him went a chiffon sari that rose in the wind. Ramesh was afraid that the wind would strip off her sari any moment and leave her naked.

'This world is so beautiful,' Suja who was walking through the fields with the wind lifting her hair and her sari, said.

'As beautiful as you,' Avinash added.

There were guava trees here and there. Avinash picked a few guavas hanging on low branches and held them out to Suja. She started biting into the cool fruits with her even teeth. Ramesh did not eat them. He did not like fruits. If there had been chilli bushes there, he would have been very happy!

'My house!' Avinash pointed out.

It was a huge building surrounded by thick walls. Women and children came out of the huts of the village. The menfolk who were playing cards sitting on the charpoys – cots with woven webbing – outside stopped their game and looked at the guests. Some children followed them. To them Ramesh and Suja must seem like creatures from another planet.

Someone came running and opened the gate. There was a huge yard, as big as a playground, within the walls. Bullocks with humps like that of a camel stood in the yard, chewing the cud.

'One, two, three…,' Suja counted the bulls.

They walked and walked as it was quite a big yard.

'One, two, three…,' Suja counted the steps to the veranda.

There was a huge carved bedstead on the veranda. An old man sat leaning against some piled-up pillows and smoked a hookah.

'My father,' Avinash introduced him. The old man opened eyes that were like the hills created by termites and looked at Ramesh and Suja.

'Namaste, children,' he folded his hands and greeted them.

'They've come from Delhi. They're staying in our hotel.'

Avinash said that proudly. The old man opened his

toothless mouth and smiled. Someone brought a few chairs from inside. Even before they could sit, huge bronze glasses filled with lassi, the yoghurt-based drink of the area, arrived. Ramesh sipped the lassi and looked around. The wall in front was built with arches. There were four huge wooden pillars to bear the weight of the arches. Each pillar must have been a whole tree. The door leading inside was also made of thick wood.

'Avinash, your house is a palace.'

'A palace? There isn't even electricity in this place.'

These beautifully carved doors, thick pillars, arches, a yard as big as a playground…why would anyone need electricity?

'Come, come inside.'

They left the empty bronze glasses on the floor outside and got up. There was a broad hall inside the doorway. On the floor was spread a faded carpet. There were curtained rooms on all four sides of the hall. Above their heads hung an old, huge chandelier. The walls held portraits in oil and some photographs.

'Oh Phoolrani!' Avinash looked towards the interior and called out. She replied as though from a place miles away. There was the cry of a small child from behind the curtains.

'My wife. And my youngest,' Avinash explained when Phoolrani came with a child in her arms.

She was wearing a loose silk salwar and kameez stitched the old-fashioned way. Her neck and arms were covered with jewellery. A pale, unhealthy-looking young girl. No one would guess that she had three children.

Silk-clad, jewel-covered Phoolrani seemed the ghost of a princess to Ramesh.

'She won't wear a sari however much I tell her,' Avinash smiled, hiding his discontent with his unfashionable wife. Phoolrani had nothing to say. She fiddled with the child's dress and looked away. When the child started crying again, she vanished behind the curtains.

'She's the daughter of a rich landlord from Saranpur. Her father owns five tractors. Would you guess that when you look at her?'

'Yes, Avinash, your wife is a queen.'

She was a queen in Suja's eyes. Phoolrani – the queen of flowers. A name with meaning. She was a queen and this house was a palace. Ramesh looked at the ceiling with its carvings, from which the chandelier hung. A wooden ceiling. Huge doors of wood. Thick pillars carved out of wood, arches. Many curtained rooms.

He dreamed of walking through each of those rooms, moving aside the curtains.

They heard the sound of anklets beyond one of the curtains. Feet showed under the curtain. Fair fingers fiddled with the edge of the door outside the curtain.

'My sister – Urmila,' Avinash introduced her. Ramesh saw nothing except the fingers and the feet below the curtain.

They sat on cane chairs placed in the yard. Slowly the wheat fields became covered with darkness. The ban plants and the guava trees became shadows. Light from the chandelier came through the wooden pillars and doors.

Avinash got up and went in for something.

'Suja, we are in the past now. We are going backwards in time. This bungalow with its chandelier is a memory from the past. These pillars that stand in a row, those arches, they all point the way to the past. Suja, don't you see the mystery of the past frozen behind these curtains?'

'I do see it, Ramesh.'

'Phoolrani died long ago. This old man who sits and smokes a hookah among the bolsters is also dead. The girl whose anklets tinkled behind the curtain is a ghost. Do you hear me, Suja?'

'Yes, I do. We are in the midst of ghosts wearing anklets and dupattas in a bungalow that belongs to the past, right Ramesh?'

'Yes, and if we were also dead…'

'I'm longing to come here and stand behind the curtain wearing anklets, Ramesh.'

'If only I could sit among the bolsters, close my decaying eyes and smoke a hookah…'

Avinash Arora came through the pillars, bearing a huge hookah in his hand.

'Just try this,' he held out the hookah to Ramesh.

It was an ancient hookah, worked with silver. So many generations must have enjoyed their smoke through this hookah. Ramesh took the hookah and started inhaling the smoke through the pipe that had felt the lips of so many dead people.

'Nothing for me?'

'Girls can't smoke a hookah. You can eat bhuttas if you like.'

A servant came with a cane basket filled with corn cobs. The corn cobs which had been heated in the fire were gold in colour.

An ancient bungalow. A yard into which the light of

chandeliers fell. A girl wearing a blue chiffon sari in that dim light, holding a golden corn cob in her hand.

The tinkling of the bells round the necks of the white bulls that stood in a row near the wall.

'Suja, if you and I had been alone here…'

'If we had been alone?'

'Among these thick pillars, between these greying walls, amidst these pale curtains, over the faded carpet, I would have loved you all the time…'

'After food now.' Avinash came and took the hookah from Ramesh's hands and left it on the ground. They walked into the hall. Serving plates and vessels had been spread on the table.

Beyond the curtain, the sight of fast-moving legs wearing anklets.

'Avinash, may I marry Urmila?'

'I don't mind.' He looked at Suja and laughed. 'And what will you do with her, Ramesh?'

'Strangle her.'

'This poor girl?'

Suja laughed as she ate the corn on the cob.

'Enough.' Avinash took the corn cob from her and kept it on a corner of the table. They sat around the table. A servant came and poured clear water that smelled of rose petals from an earthen pot into their glasses. As they ate, the curtains moved and beyond them feet with anklets moved in a hurry.

The light of the chandeliers spread over the ceramic and crystal bowls. Avinash served a pulao smelling of ghee and yellow carrots.

'Eat, friends.' His hands moved over the countless vessels

that had been filled with various curries...

After the main course, kulfi and rasagulla came as desserts.

'Avinash, the kulfi in Moti Mahal has to yield place to your kulfi.'

Ramesh who did not like sweets started spooning the sweet kulfi into his mouth with a silver spoon.

A child cried beyond the curtains. They heard the strains of a lullaby from somewhere. In the distance, the sound of anklets came and went. Moonlight spread outside.

'The dinner was sumptuous, Avinash.'

Ramesh sank into a cane chair under the sky of moonlight and starlight, silver-cased hookah in hand. Avinash had only one regret. There had been no meat or fish for supper. All the members of the family were vegetarians.

They heard the horn of the car from beyond the guava trees and ban plants.

'I don't feel like leaving this place, Suja.'

'Me neither, Ramesh.'

'I won't get up from this chair, ever.'

Ramesh spread his long legs and leaned further back in the chair. Suja picked up the half-eaten corn cob again.

The horn of the car sounded again. Avinash dressed and came out. He now wore a tie and had smoothed his hair with hair cream. Ramesh put down the hookah. Suja got up from her chair. It was time for them to go.

'We're going,' they made their farewells.

Phoolrani who stood leaning against the pillar, dupatta covering her face, nodded. Urmila's pale feet came and stood beyond the curtains. The old man had not woken up from his doze.

'Will you come again?' Avinash put his arms around Ramesh's shoulders and asked as they walked.

'We'll come again. One day.'

'When?' Avinash walked closer to Ramesh.

'For our honeymoon.'

Avinash's arm slipped from around Ramesh's shoulder. He stopped suddenly.

'Aren't you married?'

'No.'

'But you wrote in the register that you were?'

That was true, they had written Mr and Mrs Ramesh Panikkar in the register.

'I was standing in future time when I wrote that, my friend.'

They got into the car. Chandeliers, curtains, feet wearing anklets, give us leave to go.

Ten

'What is this, Ramesh?' Suja came out into the veranda with a closed envelope and asked. She had got it from Ramesh's suitcase. There was no address on the envelope.

'Open it and read it,' he said without removing the pipe from his mouth. It was a letter he had written to his mother some time back. He'd thought he'd post it after showing it to Suja and had forgotten all about it in the rush to get to Haridwar.

'Can I read it?'

'Definitely.'

What would her face look like when she read it? Wouldn't her eyes open wide? Wouldn't she dance with happiness?

'My dear mother…' Suja opened the envelope and started reading.

'I'm coming home during the Christmas vacation to bring you back with me. Suja and I do not want to wait any more. You must come and get the auspicious deed done. Suja's daddy will write to you about this.' She finished reading the letter. He sat and looked as her eyes opened wider and wider.

'Why didn't you post it?'

'I thought I'd do it after I showed you the letter.'

He took the letter from her and added a couple of lines, 'I reached Haridwar yesterday. I don't need to tell you that Suja is with me, do I? I shall stay here and wash away all my sins. Don't you remember what is said in "Viramitrodaya"?

Gangadware kusavarte bilvakaneelaparvate
Thirthodake khalu snata punarjanmamanvidyate

(Those who come to the blue mountain Bilvaka in Kusavarta
where the Ganga enters and bathes in the sacred waters there,
will not have to go through another rebirth.)

I shall go to Kusa Ghat tonight, to the ghat of the dead. I shall sit there and think of my father...'

When he had put the letter into another envelope and pasted it down, she asked, 'Shall I go and post it?'

There was a post box nearby. He sat on the veranda and watched her go under the dimly burning streetlights.

He could hear the sound of the Mussoorie Express going through the valley. Time was precious. Tomorrow, at this time they had to go to Delhi by this same Mussoorie Express.

'I feel like going out.'

He got up and put on his shirt. She was sitting next to the pedestal lamp with a play of Peter Handel. Her hair looked golden in the light that came through the batik shade of the lamp.

'You want to go out again, Ramesh? Isn't it time you slept?'

He had not slept the previous night too. And they had been wandering the whole day. The weariness of the climb to Manasa Devi's hill had not left them.

'This is our last night in Haridwar. Come Suja.'

'Where to, Ramesh?'

'To Kusha Ghat. To pray for my father.'

She closed the book. She came out with him with her hair left loose and no slippers on her feet. She used to do that once in while in Delhi too. He always felt on those occasions that she was a Bengali girl whom he had seen in Shanti Niketan some time ago.

None of the other rooms had a light. Avinash's room too was dark. He must be fast asleep. It was nearly midnight. The whole of Haridwar was sleeping. The roads were deserted. Last night he had wandered under the influence of charas. Night was here again.

Kusha Ghat was somewhere beyond the Lower Road. He did not know the way. But they would reach there if they walked straight. Till then, he would wander from one lane to another. They walked through the grey night towards the ghat. Oh Sage Dattatreya, here we come.

They turned into one of the lanes that connected Upar Sadak and Lower Sadak. It was pitch black. On either side of the lane, the walls had peeling skins.

'Ramesh, where are you taking me?' Suja grabbed Ramesh's hand. Hadn't he wandered through this lane last night too?

'What's that?' Her grip on his hand became tighter. A dark form rose in the dark. The tip of the trident glittered. The form lifted the trident and turned towards them.

'Ramesh!'

He did not notice that blood had drained out of her face. He turned towards the form and asked, 'Chudail, do you remember me?'

There was silence for a moment. It was as though the chudail had something to say. The tongue that hung out from the mouth would not allow speech.

'Do you know who this is?'

'The creature you said you'd seen yesterday?' She seemed slightly reassured.

The street lamp on the Lower Sadak was shining. Light fell on the chudail. Suja saw the creature clearly.

Ramesh held on to Suja's shoulder and walked along the side of the lane. The chudail followed them, trident held high.

'This creature is the embodiment of all the sins of the earth. The sins washed away from the people who come here and bathe have gathered together and taken the shape of this chudail,' Ramesh murmured to himself.

The creature put out a hand towards them. Ramesh took out a rupee from his pocket. The creature's red eyes glittered. It took the money, put its hand into the skull hung round its neck, took out a few flower petals and extended them to Suja. Suja's hands trembled when she took the flowers.

The evil presence went back to the dark lane. Sin lives in the dark, is destroyed in the dark.

In Haridwar, the land of the gods, in Haridwar, the entrance to heaven, a demon also wanders with the gods. The gods were frozen idols. But the demon lives in flesh and blood and begs for food. I prefer the living demon to the frozen idols – O Trinity of gods, O great sages, forgive me!

They walked through the narrow Lower Sadak, passing the closed shops. It was very quiet. They could hear the sound of the Ganga flowing in the distance.

'Ramesh, let's go back.' Suja was feeling scared. It was past midnight. The road was unfamiliar and deserted.

'Don't be afraid, child,' Ramesh lit a cigarette, held her close to his body and continued his journey. Countless devotees come and go in Haridwar. They bathe in the Ganga, visit the temples and go back. How many of them would have tried to find the real Haridwar? How many of them would have seen the chudail? Haridwar had a number of faces. One face for daylight, another for the night. The face one saw in Brahma Kund was not the face one saw in the sabjimandi, the vegetable market.

He wanted to see all the nooks and corners of Haridwar before he returned to Delhi. He wanted to expose the faces of this land of gods that none had seen before. Suja's fear faded after a while. They held hands and walked through the lanes.

The Ganga flowed on the left side of the lane. It flowed, touching the lane. A drain which came from the right cut across the lane and fell into the river. A small distance away from where the water from the drain fell into the river, they could see the dome of a temple among high walls. Whose temple was it? They walked towards it.

The door to the temple was open. It led to a long yard paved with stones. They could see people sleeping here and there on stringed cots. Turned away from them, facing the river, there were three temples.

As they walked through the yard, their footsteps echoed like drumbeats in the silence.

They stood between the river and the temples. The temple at the right end was covered with moss. Still, the murals had not faded away completely. There were doves that rubbed their beaks together. On the other side were peacocks who seemed about to tear each other to pieces. One normally saw peacocks who had spread their feathers and were about to dance. It was the first time the two of them saw peacocks whose eyes held anger.

The heavy doors were shut and they could not see the idol. They could not see the idol in the small temple in the middle either. They moved to the temple on the left side. There were no murals or carvings there. There was just a dilapidated idol in the temple. Since the face and head were eroded they could not make out whose idol it was. Oh, god with the unknown name, we bow before you…

They sat with their backs to the deserted temples. In front of them lay the river, pale in the moonlight. Fish danced in the water. With their faces resting on their knees, they sat looking at the Ganga. Oh Ganga, who released the sixteen thousand sons of Emperor Sagara from their sins, won't you forgive me my small errors? Won't you wash away my small sins? As she flowed over the marks made by the chariot of Bhageeratha, was the river smiling?

'Ramesh!'

'Umm?'

'Why aren't you saying anything?'

'I'm thinking.'

He was thinking: what are these experiences that I am going through? At the age of eight I lighted my father's pyre. Even before I graduated to long trousers, I had started smoking opium and going to prostitutes, making my mother's eyes weep without a pause. Last winter I'd gone to Señor Herozi and picked a fight in a bar. Six months earlier, I'd been admitted to the hospital with an overdose of bhang and spent three days fighting with death. All that was me. And now, I sit in Haridwar, at midnight, amidst deserted temples with this lovely girl.

What is this I!

'I'll go to sleep if I sit here for a little longer,' Suja's head dipped towards Ramesh's chest. 'Look for lice in my hair.'

Ramesh sat searching for non-existent lice in her hair. She started humming a song softly. The Ganga flowed quietly before them. The silent temples were bathed in moonlight. They were the yaksha and yakshini who had lost their way. His fingers that had been searching for lice moved down to her neck with its soft down of hair. His hands caressed her ribs under her blouse. Your body where I find my own warm smell…

The yaksha and yakshini became one between the Ganga and the deserted temples, in the moonlight. Oh gods with unknown names, Gangadevi, forgive us…

'Suja, Dattatreya is calling me. I have to pray for my father.'

Ramesh left the grounds through the open door. Suja followed him like a shadow. They moved through the lanes again. Somewhere in the faint darkness of the lane they heard the sound of a bell and saw a white shadow. The white cow walked slowly and came up to the wall.

'What is it, cow? Don't you have to sleep at all? I gave the chudail money. What shall I give you?'

The cow held its ears up and lifted its face towards him.

'Isn't this the cow you said you saw yesterday?'

'Yes. But this is not just a cow. It is the embodiment of virtue.'

The white cow that was the soul of Haridwar wandered

through the night, jingling the bells hung around its neck.

They stood under the arches at the Kusha Ghat. Pandas, the priests, curled up and slept on the steps. This ghat was where the offerings to the dead were made. The bones of so many people flowed away here. One could see the dead leaf lamps float here and there in the water.

My dear father, who died one evening, bleeding from blood vessels that had burst open, I remember you... I pray for you...

They sat under the arch, looking at the river. The sound of Bhageeratha's chariot could be heard distantly. The voice of Gangadevi.

> *Darsayaswa maharaja margam kena vrajamyaham...*
> (Oh king, show me the way forward...)

Gangadevi followed the chariot of Bhageeratha as it moved through the valleys of Kailas. The sons of Sagara who wandered as lost souls in Haridwar were about to obtain salvation.

Bhageeratha's chariot passed the Triveni, the confluence of three rivers at Rishikesh, and reached Haridwar. Neither Bhageeratha nor Gangadevi saw the Sage Dattatreya who had been doing severe penance on one leg for decades. Bhageeratha's chariot passed by the sage, loud and triumphant. The kusha grass that had been collected by Dattatreya for his rituals was washed away by the Ganga. Sage Dattatreya opened his eyes and saw the river Ganga sweeping away his gatherings. Gangadevi trembled before the angry eyes of the divine sage. When Dattatreya was about to burn Gangadevi, Bhageeratha fell at Brahma's feet and sought his intervention.

If the Ganga were destroyed, the sixteen thousand sons of Emperor Sagara would never attain salvation.

'Forgive them just this once,' Lord Brahma came down to earth and pleaded with Sage Dattatreya. 'The Trimurti will stand guard over your penance till it's over – so that there is no interruption.'

Dattatreya calmed down and pardoned Gangadevi. The Trimurti stood guard over Dattatreya at Kusha Ghat for a thousand and one years, till he had completed the penance.

I'm standing at the place where Sage Dattatreya performed a penance for a thousand and one years. I'm standing at the place where the Trimurti, the trinity of gods had stood. Ramesh stood stunned, mind and body thrilled at the thought.

'All my sins are burning, Suja. I can't bear the heat of this fire.'

He was sweating even in the cool breeze that wafted from the Ganga.

'Come on, let's go.'

When they reached the Upar Sadak, the sky had paled. They could hear the sound of a conch from somewhere.

Eleven

Hanuman pedalled away to Kankhal. Ramesh and Suja were in the rickshaw. When you watched Hanuman stand on the pedals and press them down, you felt that he was a horse – a horse that ran tossing its hair, stamping hard on the ground.

'Hanuman!'

'Yes, Memsaab?'

'You are dead.'

Hanuman turned around and looked at Suja with a start.

'Do you know how you died? You died of blood cancer.'

'Don't say such things, Memsaab. It's a sin to talk like that. I have a wife and children,' he pleaded.

'I'll take care of your wife and children, that's all right then, isn't it?'

'Memsaab!' his voice was pleading.

'Anyway, how would you have a wife and children once you are dead? Dead people don't have families. They have no one. Death means freedom, Hanuman. You are lucky to be dead!'

Hanuman suddenly put on the brakes. The rickshaw swayed and shook. It had nearly hit a horse-drawn cart, inviting curses from the driver.

'What've you done, Hanuman?'

'You can't blame him. If you look a man in the face and tell him that he's dead, he's bound to be upset, Suja.'

When Hanuman started pedalling again, Suja reassured him, 'Hanuman, you aren't dead, not really.'

The rickshaw stopped a little distance away from the Daksheswara Mahadev temple at Kankhal. They got down from the rickshaw and looked around. The Daksheswara temple was in front of them. Daksheswar, here we stand in your divine presence…

The temple was ancient with a narrow entrance. They entered it and saw the old Sivalinga. They scattered the flowers they had brought with them over it.

'Daksheswar, we have not forgotten Satidevi. We have brought flowers for your beloved wife too.'

Daksheswar, we bid farewell.

Daksha Prajapati, here we come.

It was a small temple with a pot-shaped dome on top and entrances on all sides. They entered through an arch.

Daksha Prajapati, the Puranas and Vedas might hate you but I do not. Your arrogance is the arrogance of mankind. Though many Dwapara Yugas have passed, your ego still stands. I hear the sound of the Sivajwaras, the spirits let loose by Siva, all around me.

Daksha Prajapathi, my fate, the fate of mankind, is your fate. It is no wonder that the yajna, the fire sacrifice started by you could not be completed. My whole life consists of yajnas that had to be left incomplete.

Oh son of Lord Brahma, we still keep faith in you, the

seed of all human life. There's Vietnam, there's Biafra, there are the Arabs and the Jews.

We gaze towards Kailas, in expectation of our destruction. Waiting for the arrival of Virabhadra and the spirits sent by Siva. Let the Satidevis continue to burn in the sacrificial fire. It is our fate…

Ramesh felt that the journey to Kankhal was not just a journey from one place to another. It was a journey through time. A journey from one manuantara to another manuantara. Manuantara literally means the life span of Manu, the Hindu progenitor of humanity. There are fourteen manuantaras in the current aeon, each under a Manu. With the end of Daksha, Chakshusha manuantara ended and Vaivasvata manuantara, the present universe, started. When the spirits sent by Siva pierce the eyes of Pusha and Bhaga, a new manuanthara is born.

❖

Lost between Chakshusha and Vaivasvata manuantaras, Ramesh walked along.

The rickshaw moved through Kankha Jwalapur. It stopped before the Sati Kund.

This was where the fire sacrifice of Daksha Prajapati took place. This was where Satidevi threw herself into the sacrificial fire and died.

They rested under a tree. Hanuman sat in the rickshaw, smoking a beedi.

Sitting at the Sati Kund, Suja lying with her head on his lap, Ramesh asked, 'Do you know the story of the sage called Kandu?'

'Who is sage Kandu?'

'Sage Kandu performed penance for years and years, immersed in water. The gods were made nervous by such piety and sent an apsara, a divine nymph called Pramlocha, to distract him. Pramlocha was exceedingly beautiful and managed to attract Kandu. She made him forget his penance and lived with him. They spent nine hundred and seven years, six months and three days in love-play. When it was time for Pramlocha to return to the world of gods, Kandu, who was still lost in love, pleaded with her to stay back. But she had to go. Kandu was angered by what he saw as Pramlocha's stubbornness. Fire flowed out of his eyes. Frightened by his anger, Pramlocha fled to the world of gods through air. The leaves of trees wiped her sweat as she fled. Through the sweat wiped by them, Pramlocha's pregnancy was transferred to the leaves.

'The wind and the moon collected the traces of pregnancy from the leaves of trees and created the beautiful girl called Marisha.'

Ramesh smoothed the hair of the girl who had kept her head on his lap to the side and concluded the story, 'Prajapati Daksha is the son of Marisha.'

They got up when they felt rested and started walking – through Mayapuri that had known the footfalls of Satidevi.

'Did you see everything, Babuji?' Hanuman who had been dozing in the rickshaw woke up and asked.

'We saw everything, my friend. We saw Virabhadra create an army from his hair follicles. We saw the cut head of Daksha and the body with its new sheep-head. We saw the destroyed palace of Daksha.'

The rickshaw moved again. Here I return from Chakshusha

manuantara to the Vaiasvata manuantara...

Next, they went to the Anjanadevi temple. And from there to the distant Satyanarayana temple.

There were so many temples! So many gods and goddesses!

'Suja, I think there are more gods and goddesses in Haridwar than human beings.'

'Ramesh, if only you had been a god and I a goddess...!' Suja could not help wishing.

The Satyanarayana temple was seven miles away from Arora's hotel. The sun was already high in the sky. Huge temples stood crowding together under the dark blue sky, in the bright sunlight. These temples were larger and more beautiful than all the temples they had seen anywhere else in Haridwar.

'Suja, the grandeur of the Satyanarayana temple is flowing into me.'

'I liked the Anjanadevi temple.'

She liked the deserted Anjanadevi temple that did not have any worshippers, that had no lamps or flowers.

'What if someone built a temple for me?'

'Even then I shall like the Anjanadevi temple.'

'So, you care more for Anjanadevi than for me?'

'Ramesh, you are a part of me. So, when I like a temple, you should like it too, shouldn't you?'

'I like the Daksha temple best.'

'Ramesh, yours is a dual existence. You live in yourself and me at the same time.'

'Nobody has an existence that is special to themselves.'

'They do.'

'No, they don't.'

'They do. Suppose no one exists in this world but me. Then my existence will be mine alone.'

'When you stand against the wind you are partaking of the life of that wind, aren't you? Don't you enter the life of air when you breathe the air? When you walk and small insects die under your foot, don't you exist in them too? You idiot, are you arguing with me?'

'All right, I give up.'

She leaned her head against his shoulder.

Twelve

He needed some ganja or charas. It was more than twenty-four hours since he had had a fix. Nothing like this had happened in the recent past. Ramesh was feeling very restless.

It was not that he did not know that intoxicants were banned in Haridwar. But they were banned in Delhi too. How did that matter? You could get charas or ganja or opium in any quantities there. He was not fool enough to believe that you could not get these things in Haridwar.

He paced the veranda restlessly for a long time. Finally, he decided to take a risk and got out of the room. He would go up to the sabjimandi and try. If he got something, well and good. If he could at least get raw arrack that would be a help. He had to wet his throat. That was all. If he could not do that at least, he might even descend to madness.

The sun was burning down hotly. The moment he got out on to the road, the sides of his head and his armpits were covered with sweat. He met a hippie in front of the post office, a solitary man who had lost his companions. He was walking, looking to either side in turn, worried and upset. He could be carrying something…

But a disappointment awaited him there. The man was carrying nothing.

'You don't have to give it to me for free. I can pay you.'

He was ready to give him anything. For some opium, he was willing to give any person the four-hundred-rupee watch he wore on his wrist. The hippie shrugged.

Ramesh walked along the side of the road, where the shadows of the trees fell. This was the main street. There were plenty of people. There were policemen. It was not likely that he would get any drugs here.

He went into the inner sanctums of Haridwar through Bhalla Road. There might even be ganja cultivation in one of these dark streets. He wondered how many secrets were hidden in these inner areas.

After walking for a while, he thought to himself: there is no point in walking aimlessly. He had to work up the courage to ask someone. He chose a sweetmeat vendor. The man's eyes were like that of a bhang addict.

'Lalaji!'

His heavy eyes fell on Ramesh.

'Come, come!' Lala invited Ramesh. He took out the balance and straightened out the tangled strings.

'Lalaji, please don't get angry, I want some opium.'

Lalaji returned the balance to its resting place on his hips. His face flamed with anger. That was when Ramesh noticed the pictures and idols of gods and goddesses all over the shop. A red bulb burned before a picture of Srigangaji that was decked with flower garlands.

'Suvar! You pig!' He heard the shopkeeper say from behind as he walked away.

Pig – Yes, I'm a dirty pig.

'Police, police – catch him,' that was Lala's voice. Ramesh had turned into another lane before the attention of the people could turn towards him.

He saw a medicine shop in sabjimandi. There were roots and leaves tied up in bunches. An almirah was chock-a-block with bottles of vividly coloured medicines and jars with various paste-like concoctions.

He was sure they would have something here. If he could not get ganja, there would at least be arrack.

The vaid, the physician, politely asked him to sit down. Ramesh did not sit down but told him what he'd come in search for. The physician ran his eyes behind spectacles over Ramesh.

'Son, this is Haridwar.'

'Don't you have anything at all? Usually medical shops like this stock bhang to make medicines. Give me a little from that at least.'

'May god forgive you.' The physician removed his glasses and kept them on his lap.

Ramesh got out of the shop. At least, this man had not called the police. Small mercies.

A mendicant was sitting beside the road behind Har Ki Pauri. In front of him was a picture of Gayatri Devi, an incarnation of Saraswati Devi. He was reciting something tunefully. There were small coins in the saffron piece of cloth before him.

When he put a one-rupee coin in the cloth, the mendicant's recital stopped.

'Swamiji!'

'What is it, my son?'

Ramesh bent before the mendicant and asked in a soft voice, 'Do you have any ganja?'

'May the Lord Sankara save you from sinful thoughts.' The mendicant took a handful of water and threw it at Ramesh's face.

Ramesh took out his handkerchief, wiped his face and walked again. The lanes near Har Ki Pauri were all crowded. The shops on either side seemed heaped together. Costume jewellery, glass bangles, sindoor, small idols, swords, tridents, conches, bells...

He did not see anything. He did not even feel the touch of the people who passed him as though in a procession. He had just one thought in his mind. A piece of ganja. Or a drop of arrack.

When he noticed the face of the middle-aged man who sat on the steps leading from the Lower Sadak to the ghats, he felt relieved. It was a face that he knew from G.B. Road in Delhi – all brokers had the same face. Anyone who knew the type could pick them up from any crowd.

'Ayiye, Babuji, please come, sir...'

The voice was that of a woman. Ramesh walked after him. When they reached a deserted lane, the broker asked, 'Kya cheez chahiye? What stuff do you want?'

'Kya cheez hai tere pas? What stuff do you have?'

The man stayed silent for a moment and then said in his effeminate voice, 'There are girls as pretty as birds.'

'Can I get something to drink?'

'What do you want, Babu?'

'Bhang.'

'Ayiye! Come with me!'

The lane reminded one of nothing so much as hell. The way led through a shop selling betel leaves and areca nuts. The door was covered by a curtain on which dirt lay in thick layers. Ramesh went through the curtain behind the broker.

'Where's Goli? That stupid girl! Oh Goli!'

A girl came from inside. She would have been fifteen or sixteen. Her breasts were just forming.

'See Babuji, isn't she pretty?' The broker brought Goli forward to stand before Ramesh.

When the end of the sari that had covered her head slipped down, Ramesh saw the mark of vermillion in the parting. Her cheeks were pale and lips red with the chewing of betel leaves. She wore silver anklets.

'Draw her close, Babuji,' the broker patted him on the shoulder and said.

Ramesh extended his hand and touched her arm with its red glass bangles.

'She's my only child. Don't get me wrong Babuji, it's only because there's nothing else I can do.'

'You can go.'

'Look child, make Babuji happy. He's from the city. He's got lots of money and lots of degrees.'

The man withdrew slowly. Standing on the threshold, he called out just before he vanished, 'Your drink will be ready immediately. Just five minutes.'

'Sit here.'

Goli smiled without lifting her head. She glanced at Ramesh through the corner of her eye and pulled up the end of the sari to cover her head again.

As he sat and looked at her he forgot all about the ganja for the time being. He pulled her to his lap and caressed her hair that held the smell of the soil. Not just her hair, the whole of her had the smell of rain-soaked earth. A girl who smelled of the earth.

'Goli, give this to the Babuji,' the effeminate voice sounded from behind the curtain.

'Coming, Bapu.'

She picked up the sari that was lying on the ground and pulled it round her anyhow and went to the doorway. She came back with a green liquid in a big cup with a broken edge. When he saw it, he acted desperate like a bird that had seen water suddenly.

He shut his eyes tight and swallowed the contents of the cup in one gulp. This was not bhang mixed with milk and almonds and cooled in the refrigerator. How had Goli's Bapu prepared this? Who knew? When he put the cup down he felt as though he would throw up everything, even his intestines. He rubbed his mouth hard with the back of his hand and lighted a cigarette.

Goli went to the door and bolted it then.

She started unbuttoning Ramesh's shirt as he lay there on the coir cot. The red bush shirt with black checks that Suja had given him for his last birthday…

As the charpoy creaked, the womanish voice sounded from beyond the door, 'Are you making Babuji happy, child?'

'Yes, Bapu.'

Ramesh was waiting for his throat to get dry and for his muscles to loosen up. But nothing happened. Only the sickeningly bitter taste of the bhang remained in his mouth.

Was that liquid he had made him drink, bhang? Or had he been tricked?

Ramesh walked through the heat of the midday, waiting for the effect of the bhang. Nothing happened. He wondered whether he should go back and get another cup of it to drink. He became more and more restless as time passed. There was a whistling sound somewhere in his brain. The whistling sound that came when he had not used alcohol or drugs for a long time. The beginning of madness.

He bought sweet laddus from a shop on the way and ate them. Sweetness gave power to bhang. Nothing happened still. Oh god! I shall go mad if this continues…

'Babuji! What are you doing here, Babuji?' Hanuman came closer to Ramesh, pedalling his rickshaw.

'Hanuman! I need some arrack. Tell me, where can I get some?'

'Babuji!…'

'Hanuman, I had some bhang. But nothing happened. I think that Goli's Bapu cheated me. Hanuman, I must drink something. Tell me, where do I have to go to get a little arrack?'

'Babuji…'

Ramesh got into the rickshaw. The heat of the midday sun was burning in his head. The air he breathed was hot as embers.

Hanuman pedalled the rickshaw forward. The streets were unfamiliar. Finally they went into a lane and Hanuman knocked on a door there.

Someone brought out a green liquid.

'We call this Bhagda, Babuji.'

Hanuman explained. If the colour of the dusk was orange and the colour of Jagadari red, Bhagda was coloured green. Hanuman tilted the bottle. As Ramesh brought the glass closer to his mouth, his throat dried up and his limbs felt weak. The bhang was beginning to work.

Hanuman drank only a little. It was Ramesh who emptied the bottle.

'Come, Babuji, I'll take you to the hotel.' Hanuman walked towards the rickshaw.

'I'm not going to the hotel. I want to wander a little all alone, Hanuman.'

'Babuji!'

'Go away, Hanuman.'

When the rickshaw was moving away, Ramesh shouted after it, 'Thank you, Hanuman, thank you very much!'

But did any sound come out?

He did not know which streets he was walking through. He must have traversed a number of lanes. He saw the crowds in Har Ki Pauri as though in a dream.

When he came to himself he was standing near Bhimgoda. After a moment, he lost his senses again. This wandering in the unconscious state took him here and there. When he came to himself again, he was sitting on a milestone on the Rishikesh road. His body was heavy as granite. Was he an idol? He could not move his body. He tried to make his hands move. He could not.

Yes, he was an idol. He had changed into stone due to a curse cast by a sage. Ramesh suddenly felt afraid. Would he have to remain a statue all his life? Was there an antidote to this?

Suja would be waiting for him. Wouldn't she get worried when he did not get back? They had to return by the ten o'clock express at night. Wouldn't she come in search of him when he did not turn up? When she saw him sitting like this, frozen into a statue, on the Rishikesh road, wouldn't she cry aloud? Ramesh's eyes welled up when he thought of that.

His throat was so parched he felt it would crack. He needed some water. He needed to put his head down and sleep somewhere. But he could not move his tongue. This was to be his fate – to spend the whole of his life as a granite statue, unable to speak or move.

Ramesh remembered that he had taken bhang and the strong arrack named bhagda on top of it. So, this feeling that he had frozen into a statue was probably just an illusion. Even before he could finish that thought, lava flowed through his throat. He squatted on the side of the road. When he got up after five minutes, vomit lingered on his chin and his chest.

He continued to walk aimlessly on the Rishikesh Road. Every now and then, he squatted on the side of the road. Buses with pilgrims to Badrinath passed by, almost touching him.

He could hear the sound of the Saptadhara in his ears. How did I reach here? For what did I come here? Oh Saptarishis, the seven divine sages, did you call me here? He removed his slippers and entered the Paramatmasram. And then he went in and out of the temples. As he stood at the Durga temple, he held on to the wall strongly to prevent himself from falling. The walls around him were made of mirrors. The hanging lamps with their flaming wicks created a flood of light around him.The idol of the Mahamaya with a blood-stained trident. A roaring tiger beside her.

One could not enter the temple. Feeling giddy, he held on tight to the parapet and peered inside. On either side were rows of innumerable idols and lamps that stretched into infinity. He could not make out that this was done with mirrors. His brain and his reasoning faculty were numb.

Once again he could hear the roar of the Saptadhara in his ears. As he entered the Saptakshetra, the temple to the seven sages, the roar became muted. Idols of the great sages stood inside the temple. The sacrificial fire continued to burn.

The silence was frightening. There were no human beings or horses on the dirt track outside. There were only the footsteps left behind by them. There were rails that stretched endlessly.

Ramesh could see the first human being born in the island of Krauncha. The soul in its airy form that had been born of the shadow of the pitrs spread from Krauncha to the island of Kusha and from there to the island of Satmala. Aeons passed. The son of Chakshus took the reins of the Manuantara, the change of aeons from the hands of Raivata, the brother of Tamasata and drove the chariot through the kalpas. Finally, Vaivaswata took birth, sounding the birth of a new Manuantara.

This manuantara, his manuantara, the manuantara of Ramesh Panikkar.

At the end of the Treta Yuga, Havishman, Viraka, Sumedhas, Uthaman, Madhu, Atinama, Asahishnu became Vasishta and Viswamitra.

Traversing seventy-one Satya Yugas, seventy-one Treta Yugas, and seventy-one Dwapara Yugas, wandering through twenty-seven Kali Yugas, the human soul that was born in

Krauncha Dweep, stands before you, O Great Sages, in the form of Ramesh Panikkar. In the previous manuantara, in the palace of Mantradyumna, who had I been, under what name had I sought your sacred feet, O sages?

'My limbs do not have the strength to carry me through another forty-three Kali Yugas. O saviour of my kalpa, take birth, give me salvation,' he thought.

In the silence of time, in the darkness of wisdom, under the sacred kachnar tree, Ramesh sat half-unconscious. He could hear the curse of Sage Kapila from the time of Ikshwaku. Ganga, who had followed Bhageeratha from heaven, had become imprisoned by the seven divine sages here. Bhageeratha fell at the feet of the sages. He pleaded – don't let the terrible penance I did for the salvation of my ancestors go waste. The seven sages took pity on the human and released Ganga. Bhageeratha led Ganga to Haridwar. The sons of Sagara, the ancestors of Bhageeratha, felt the touch of Ganga and were released from their sins to attain heaven.

Aeons passed.

Even today, when the Ganga reaches the presence of the sages, she splits into seven and makes her obeisance at the seven hermitages. After that, the seven streams join and flow as one to Haridwar.

Ramesh stood on the soil that witnesses this drama again and again. Before him flowed the seven Gangas.

He walked back through the frightening emptiness of the riverside. He saw only mendicants who had left behind everything in life. Upar Sadak and Avinash's hotel and Suja were far away. Would he reach there? His ears still rang with the sound of the chariots of the emperors from the old manuantaras. Treta Yuga falls away and Dwapara Yuga is born. Again and again. Newer yugas, newer incarnations and the seven sages. The yugas become mahayugas and manuantaras become chaturdasa manuantaras...

What was the end of this great drama? Oh my god!

When his legs gave way, he fell on the road with a cry that would not come out of his mouth.

Thirteen

Suja was packing clothes and other things in the suitcase. She was preparing for the journey. Ramesh sat and looked on through half-closed eyes. He could not do anything. He was in such a state that he could not even sleep.

Suja pointed to the ash-coloured trousers and handloom shirt that lay on the bed and said, 'Ramesh these are for you to wear now.' She shut both the suitcases. She wondered if he'd heard what she said.

They only had a few more hours in Haridwar. Three days had passed so fast – faster than three hours did normally. For the past three days this room had been their home. What had this room not witnessed? Didn't the smell of burnt charas still linger in the room? This room had witnessed their love-making. Their tears had fallen on this carpet…

Someone else would occupy this room once Ramesh and Suja left. Would the play they had acted out here be repeated by those others? Would the tears of a young woman fall here again? Would smoke from charas again fill the space between these walls?

Hanuman was standing below on the street, leaning against his cycle rickshaw.

'Ramesh.'

He tried to open his eyes.

'Change your clothes. Hanuman is waiting for us.'

When she insisted, he wore the trousers and shirt. As they went down the stairs he held on to the railings because he was scared he would fall.

'You must get back before 8 o'clock,' Avinash reminded them. 'The train's at ten. If you get here before eight, you can have a leisurely dinner and go to the railway station in time.'

The rickshaw moved towards Har Ki Pauri. From the hotel to the Brahma Kund was only walking distance. About three or four furlongs. But Ramesh could not walk even a step.

'Ramesh, are you asleep?' Suja shook him awake. He sat there with half-shut eyes, saying nothing. This was not the Ramesh who had gone out of the room in the afternoon. His face had shrunk like a dried fruit. His eyes were dark and hollow.

'What happened to you, Ramesh?'

She put his hand on her lap and slowly caressed it. He wanted to say a lot of things but his tongue would not move. His hand on her lap was trembling.

She had never seen him look so bad, ever.

'Ramesh!'

'Umm?'

She wanted to say a lot of things. That he should not make her so unhappy. That he should not make her shed tears every day. But when she looked at his face, she swallowed her words and sat quietly, holding his hand in both of hers.

'When is the train, Memsaab?' Hanuman asked as he pedalled.

'It's at ten, Hanuman.'

'Do you have to go today itself, Memsaab?'

'Yes.'

Her mother was waiting impatiently for her. Her daddy would have come. Señor Herozi would be waiting for Ramesh. If he did not go to the office on Monday, Señor Herozi would not be able to work. Besides, there was the chess tournament in the evening. He had reached the semi-finals. Perhaps he would be the next state champion, who knew?

Delhi was waiting for them. They could not be even a day late.

By this time the next day, they would be in Delhi. She would be in the painting class. He would be battling Amir Syed Khan on the chess board.

'Will you come to Haridwar again, Memsaab?' Hanuman's voice held sadness.

'What is there to be sad about, Hanuman? How many people do we meet in this life only to part again and forget!' said Suja to herself.

'Memsaab, will you write to me?'

'But you don't know how to read and write, Hanuman.'

Hanuman had forgotten that when he asked her to write.

The rickshaw stopped at Har Ki Pauri. It was forbidden to take vehicles right up to the ghats. The visitors who came to Brahma Kund had to stop their vehicles on the main street of Har Ki Pauri and walk the rest of the way.

'Ramesh!'

Ramesh was not sleeping though he had not uttered a word. Before his eyes were the yugas that fell away. In his ears rang the sound of the chariots of the emperors who had ruled the manuantaras.

Tameva saranam gachcha
Sarvabhavena bharata
Tatprasadat param santim
Sthanam prapyasai saswatam.
(Go to Him for refuge, with all your being,
O Arjuna. By His grace you shall obtain supreme peace and reach the eternal abode.)

The loud cry of the mendicant from Manasa Devi's hill resounded in his ears again and again.

'Ramesh, what's happened to you?' Suja shook him again. He got out of the rickshaw.

'Should I wait?'

'No, Hanuman, we'll walk back to the hotel.' She took out money from her handbag.

'No, Memsaab, there's no need.' When she held out the money, Hanuman moved backward. He got on to his rickshaw without taking the money and vanished among the crowds.

Red had spread over the distant mountain range. The sun was setting behind the hill of Manasa Devi. The ghats were getting crowded. People were flowing to the Brahma Kund through the Upar Sadak and the Lower Sadak.

They now stood at the Vishnu Ghat, which was the abode of Mahavishnu. It was here that Sage Durvasa had cursed Dharmadwaja of the Sun dynasty and turned him into a serpent. Every fourteenth day of the waning moon, the serpent comes to the Vishnu Ghat to bathe.

They saw people who had killed cows bathe at the Gau Ghat in expiation of that sin.

Ramesh walked from one ghat to another, as though he

was walking from one Kalpa to another. He forgot that there was a world beyond those ghats. He was not conscious of time or place. He walked forward with fever in his soul.

A cow that was wandering under the pauris or ghats had a number of coloured pieces of cloth wrapped around its body. There were bells round its neck. The white cow wandered among the mendicants and the pilgrims – like a soul that had achieved salvation.

Ramesh's mind yearned painfully for the purity of soul that the white cow had attained. Sins were burning in him. Weren't those the pyres of sins that burnt in his sunken eyes?

'Ramesh, you have a fever!' Her hands burned when she touched Ramesh. The fever had spread from his soul to his body. 'Let's go back.'

His eyes that seemed to be sinking every moment frightened her.

Where do we go? Where can I go from these ghats and temples?

They left their slippers outside and walked to the Brahma Kund. The pauris or paidis had been built by Vikramaditya. There were many pilgrims bathing at the ghat. Leaves of the sacred bel or wood apple tree and flowers of different kinds were lying in the water. Pujas were going on in the temples that crowded together in the water and on the shore. A sacrificial fire burned in the island in the middle of the river. Sanyasis sat around the fire throwing ghee and incense into the fire and reciting the Gayatri mantra.

The mountains darkened in the distance. Red drained out from the sky. Aratis, prayer ceremonies with lighted lamps and incense, blazed in the river. Devotees were floating leaf platters with flowers and small flames. The pilgrims who had gathered thickly on the shores pleaded for succour and recited the names of gods. Their voices lingered like a lament on the shores.

The puja was over. Thousands of leaf-held flames floated down the river. The priests who came out of the temples held high flames in their hands and went down the steps of the ghat. They stood in a row on the last step – with flames held above their heads, eyes opened towards the sky.

Bells rang continuously from the innumerable temples in Haridwar. The sound of conches from the temples echoed over the river. Some of the pilgrims who were beating their breasts and crying fell unconscious.

Ramesh stood there, stunned. His ears were filled with the sounds of conches and bells that swept in like waves. The light of the flames that were held up towards the sky turned him blind. He was burning like a sacrificial fire himself…

The flames in the temples ran out of oil. The aratis in the river floated away.The ghats were getting deserted.

❖

It was half past eight.

'Ramesh!' Suja shook him. They had only another hour and a half in Haridwar. They had to get back to the hotel. He was still burning with fever. She had to get him some medicine. And then go straight to the railway station.

'We'll miss the train if we sit around like this, Ramesh,' she reminded him. When she put her hand on his neck, it was as hot as a burning flame. He was sitting motionless, gazing at the river. The flames on the leaf platters were still flaming before his eyes. His ears were ringing with the waves of sound from the bells and the conches – still.

'Oh god! The fever will get worse if we sit like this,' Suja spoke to herself. The Brahma Kund was almost empty. The flowers and flames had floated away through the river. A few lamps that had not caught the flow lay near the steps – with flames that trembled in the wind.

'Won't you get up, Ramesh?'

'We'll go tomorrow.'

This was not his voice with which she was so familiar. She looked at him in surprise.

'Don't upset me like this, Ramesh!'

'Go!'

'Where can I go, Ramesh? Where do I go without you?' Her eyes had filled with unshed tears.

He did not reply but sat with his eyes fixed somewhere far away. The lamps in the temples had gone out. The fire in the sacrificial pit had also died out. The flames that had floated in the river were now just platters made of leaves.

'Ramesh!' Her voice had changed into a cry.

He sat motionless as an idol. She stood there not knowing what to do – for a long time. Later she too sat next to him on the step and her sobs rose in the empty ghat.

After a little while the Mussoorie Express passed through the valley of the hill, hooting.

❖

The sun rose over Haridwar.

The hotel boy picked up the suitcases and walked towards the taxi that was waiting. Avinash was standing next to the car. He wore a woollen muffler round his neck. Mornings in Haridwar carried a nip.

Suja picked up her handbag. She had bathed. Her hair that was still rather damp lay carelessly over her back. Her forehead held the usual big bindi.

She waited for Ramesh to come out. He had not washed or brushed. He got up from the bed, went to the washbasin and washed his face, wore a shirt. She had done everything that had to be done, packing, settling the hotel bills, everything.

When Ramesh had got ready, she took out a long scarf from her handbag and held it out to him, 'Wrap this round your neck, Ramesh. It's cold outside.'

He took the scarf from her and wrapped it round his neck. The Kashmir silk scarf with its red and green pattern made him look even more handsome. Ramesh went down the stairs holding on to the railings. That's when she noticed – he was not wearing his slippers.

'Ramesh, where are your slippers?'

He could not remember. She went back to the room and found his Kolhapur slippers under the washbasin. She brought them and placed them near his feet.

Avinash opened the door of the car.

'Go and meet a doctor as soon as you reach Delhi. Just taking a couple of aspirins is not enough,' he reminded Ramesh.

Ramesh had burnt with fever the whole night. It was early morning by the time the fever subsided a little. She sat near him and wiped away the sweat from his face throughout the night. Every now and then she tried to make him drink something. He had been traumatized by the fever. There were dark circles round his eyes. His already sunken eyes could not go in further.

The staff of the hotel stood there bidding a silent farewell. The car moved to the railway station. Avinash walked silently behind the porter carrying the bags. Suja held on tight to Ramesh's hands – as though she was afraid that he would run away. His palms were as cold as snow now.

Hanuman stood at the platform, smoking a beedi. When he saw Suja and Ramesh, he threw down the beedi and came towards them. He too did not say anything. He just stood there, looking at the rails.

'Will you come for Sivaratri, the festival of Siva?' Avinash asked.

Ramesh did not reply. He just stood there as though he had lost the power of speech.

'We'll come, Avinash,' Suja said.

'Write once in a while.'

'I'll write.'

The arm of the signal fell. They could hear the roar of the train in the distance.

'I shall really miss you,' said Avinash when the train reached the platform, putting his hand on Ramesh's shoulder. His voice held sadness. He and Hanuman stood on the platform and waved silently as Suja and Ramesh climbed aboard.

The train moved forward with a jerk on its innumerable wheels.

Suja looked out through the window. The train was running towards Delhi, parallel to the long road that led to Jwalapur. A long sigh rose from her without her being aware of it. She was feeling relieved at having escaped some great danger.

Daddy would have returned. Her mother would be sitting

there, eyes fixed outside. She had told them that she would reach early in the morning. Wouldn't they be anxious that they had not reached till now?

But thoughts about her mother vanished quickly from her mind. Her attention went back to Ramesh who sat leaning against the backrest next to her. Though his eyes were open, it was evident that he was not seeing anything. What was he thinking of? She did not understand. His gaze unnerved her.

'Ramesh!' She put her hand in his lap and called him. He did not reply. 'Don't frighten me like this, Ramesh.'

His silence was frightening her. This had started at the Brahma Kund yesterday. If only he would say something...

She sat with her head on his shoulder. There was no one around. If such an opportunity had arisen, would he have sat quietly at other times? She continued to sit with her head on his shoulder and gradually fell asleep.

Time passed and the train moved fast. The wheels ran a million times over the iron rails. The train passed over the endless rails, through the shores of rivers, passing Roorkee, aiming at Delhi.

Suja, who sat with her head on Ramesh's shoulder, was fast asleep. She had not shut her eyes even once the whole of the previous night. Ramesh did not sleep. He sat with his eyes open. He had been sitting like this for hours. He had not stirred even to light a cigarette in all this time. He just sat like a stone idol. He was still wandering among the kalpas, unable to find his way. His mind was still in the pit of the sacrificial fire.

Suja jerked awake once. She put her head on his lap and lay down. But she could not sleep after that. His hands were frozen cold near her face. If only those hands would move . . . if only those fingers would move through her hair . . .

When the train reached Meerut, he was still sitting with his eyes wide open.

'Ramesh!' she poured out tea from the flask. He took the cup, drank a sip and put down the cup.

They were now on the long bridge over Yamuna. Dhobi Ghat. Pyres were burning at Nigambodh Ghat. The Red Fort moved further and further backward.

She did not wash her face or tie her hair. The fear that held her mind was beginning to choke her. She waited for the train to reach the station, hair uncombed and eyes filled with tears.

She saw her driver, Syamlal, who was waiting on the platform. He came running and took their suitcases.

'Get down, Ramesh.'

'What for?'

The question had no meaning. He still spoke in that dry unfamiliar voice that he had used in the Brahma Kund.

She took him by the hand and helped him down from the train.

'Ramesh is not well. He had a fever,' she told Syamlal who was looking at her and Ramesh in turn.

She felt relieved now that her feet were firmly on the soil of Delhi. Everything that had happened seemed like a dream. Haridwar had turned into a surreal nightmare for her.

'Has daddy come, Syamlal?'

'He's come, chhoti Memsaab.'

As they got out of the station, Syamlal continued to speak, 'I had brought the car in the morning.'

'Ramesh was ill. Is my mother still angry?'

'No, chhoti Memsaab. She's been sitting with her eyes fixed outside since morning.'

She made him stop the car when they were outside Dr Nanda's clinic. She walked with Ramesh and into the clinic. The doctor was familiar with the two of them.

'Where have you two been?' Dr Nanda asked, looking at Ramesh and Suja in turn.

'We went up to Haridwar.'

'Did you see Maharshi Mahesh Yogi?'

'We didn't have time to go up to Rishikesh, Doctor.'

'How would you find time?' Dr Nanda chuckled, winking at Suja.

He led Ramesh to the bed beyond the screen and called out from there, 'Has your daddy come back from his tour?'

'Yes, doctor.'

'Mere exhaustion,' the doctor came out from behind the screen and said. Ramesh came out with his shirt buttons still undone. The doctor gave him an injection and prescribed some tablets.

'We'll go to South Extension first, Syamlal.'

'Your mother's waiting for you.'

'We'll leave immediately. Just ten minutes.'

When the car moved, she buttoned up Ramesh's shirt. She blew gently on the prick of the needle and whispered in his ear, 'Does it still hurt?'

He shook his head to say it didn't.

The car stopped in front of Ramesh's house. Syamlal took his suitcase up to his room. Suja opened the almirah and took out a pair of pyjamas for him to wear. She went to the kitchen and made tea. She made him take his tablet and drink the tea.

'I'll ring up and speak to Herozi. Don't go anywhere. Don't even get down from the bed.'

She covered Ramesh with a sheet as he lay stretched on the bed. Kneeling near the bed, she put her face against his and whispered, 'I'll be back soon. Within half an hour.'

Syamlal was waiting outside impatiently. She went down the steps, humming under her breath.

When Suja had left and he was lying all alone in the room, the sounds of the chariots of the manuantaras came back to his ears. The emptiness and silence between the yugas covered him. He sat up in the bed. When he could no longer sit, he started pacing the room. Unable to sit or sleep or even walk, he wandered about the room like a madman. Finally, he opened the door and went outside.

The telephone in the room was ringing continuously. Someone said something from behind him. Someone was calling him. Not listening to anything, wearing only the pyjamas, barefoot, he walked on. The ringing of bells from the Brahma Kund echoed in his ears. The conches were sounding. He walked forward with eyes burning like the flames held to the sky.

The sun was setting in Delhi.

When he woke up, it was morning. He was in some passenger train that went to Haridwar. He was lying curved on the floor. Around him sat mendicants and beggars. The train stopped at each station, took in more and more passengers and crawled.

His throat was parched and burning with thirst. A drop of water to drink... He lost consciousness again.

It was late evening when the train reached Haridwar. He

stood again on the soil of Haridwar. This time he was not the rich and sophisticated traveller from the big city. He was a beggar who had left everything behind.

He staggered towards the Brahma Kund like a little child learning to walk. When he reached a lane in the Lower Sadak, he stopped. He opened and shut his eyes a couple of times. The chudail lay flat, face upward under the lamp post. The red false tongue had dropped off and lay nearby. The trident too lay at a little distance. There were ants on the mouth and the half-open eyes.

He passed the dead chudail and staggered towards the Brahma Kund.

Flowers and lamps filled the river. The loud recitation of the Vedas went around the sacrificial fire. The devotees continued to beat their breasts and cry…

The priests came out of the temples with the flames held high. Conches sounded. The sound of bells was raining at the Brahma Kund.

Ramesh could never escape from these flames and this sound of bells ringing.

Never.

Savitri's Girdle

One

Meethaledath was a renowned house. The men of the family abided by truth and justice at any cost to themselves. As for the women, they would sacrifice even their lives to protect their chastity.

Presently, the tharavad or household was headed by Meethaledath Ramunni, whom one could see sitting in the gatehouse and enjoying the breeze as he read the morning paper. He was fifty years old.

'We had a proper treasure chest in this family earlier. It was full of gold ornaments – necklaces, pendants, anklets . . . There was nothing that was not there . . .' Meethaledath Ramunni thought of old times and said, 'All gone. The tharavad has fallen on bad days. What can one do? It's all fate.'

'Even if everything else has gone, the tharavad still has a name, doesn't it?'

'That's my only consolation, Achu Master. My only prayer is that, whatever happens, whatever is lost, the tharavad shouldn't lose its good name in my time.'

'Just keep your mind pure, Ramunni. God will listen to prayers from the pure of heart,' said Achu Master.

Only a year older than Ramunni, Achu Master was very

thin and looked as though he would fly if you blew at him. Seeing the barber come from a distance across the fields, he got ready to leave.

'I got a little late. Didn't shut my eyes for a moment at night. My wife was feeling feverish.'

'How long have I been telling you to take your wife to a hospital and see a doctor?'

'This is not the kind of fever that will go away with medicines and needles. It is a brahmarakshas, an evil spirit. Her mother, Pokki Amma, too was possessed by a brahmarakshas till she died.'

The barber rubbed the edge of the knife against the leather strap he carried and sharpened it.

'Why is the brahmarakshas so fond of barbers' wives?'

'That's what I too don't understand. There are also the wives of goldsmiths, washermen, blacksmiths in this village. Why doesn't the brahmarakshas want any of them?' The barber complained. He was called kunhikavuthiyyan or the 'small barber' by the people of the village because of his small size.

'You can call me kunhikavuthiyyan or any other sort of kavuthiyyan. But don't ask for time to pay me for shaving you.'

The only person in the village who paid promptly after a shave was Ramunni who, at the moment, was sitting in the inner courtyard with lather on his chin. Come rain or shine, the barber would come on time to give him a shave because of that. All the rest would ask for time. Neelakantan was the person who owed the kavuthiyyan the most money. And he had to have a haircut at least twice a month. He would catch a cold if his hair grew even a quarter of an inch. Neelakantan was a dark, strong man. He was married and had two children. The major problem of his life was the head cold he kept getting.

'The kavuthiyyathi has a problem with a brahmarakshas. Neelakantan has his head colds. Each to his own . . .,' Achu Master mumbled to himself like a philosopher. Standing in front of a small shop that belonged to Kunhappu, Achu Master was chewing betel leaves. While Kunhappu had four children, kavuthiyyan had a cow and two sheep!

'That Neelakantan is coming this way. Ramunni Mooppar, you must speak to him and get me my money,' said the kavuthiyyan, folding his knife and putting it in the box he carried. Choyi, the carpenter, had made this box forty years back from the timber of a jackfruit tree. Carpenter Choyi was no longer alive but his wife still lived.

The kavuthiyyan accepted the one anna that Meethaledath Ramunni handed him and went out of the gatehouse. Neelakantan entered it at the same time.

A lot of people visited Meethaledath's house. Each would have some request to make. If a good proposal for a match was received for a girl, no household would dare fix the wedding without talking it over with Ramunni. If drunkards squabbled outside the toddy shop, it would be Ramunni who would talk to them and quieten them down. Everyone needed Ramunni for everything.

'What's it, Neelakantan, so early in the morning? I suppose you need money, right?'

Neelakantan looked down with woebegone eyes and was silent.

'You sit here on this bench. Let me go and wash my face.'

Neelakantan came in this manner only for money and Ramunni knew that.

Ramunni washed his face with water from a spouted vessel kept there for the purpose and came out. His face was shining after the clean shave.

'How much do you owe that kavuthiyyan now, Neelakantan?'

Neelakantan's false grief started flowing down his eyes.

'Umm. How much do you want now?'

'Thousand.'

'Thousand? What is it, Neelakantan, have you gone mad?'

'It is urgent. You mustn't forsake me.'

Neelakantan looked as if he would start crying out loud. The muscles of his cheeks started trembling in preparation for the sobs that were to follow.

'My dear Neelakantan, this Meethaledath house has only the old reputation. We're left with nothing. The money box is empty.'

'Still, if you set your mind to it…'

'I don't like to say things in a roundabout way. How much have you taken from me in fives and tens? Have you returned even a paisa out of that? I shall not give you anything more…'

'You don't have to give it to me just like that,' Neelakantan took out a small bundle from the fold of his mundu, the cloth tied around his waist. 'If you don't trust me, you can keep this.'

He held out the bundle.

'What's in it?'

'Gold. The weight of three sovereigns.'

'Neelakantan, you think you can insult this Meethaledath house? What are we, a bank where you can pledge gold ornaments? Go away from here. You won't get a paisa from me.'

Meethaledath Ramunni's face went red. He went and washed his mouth once more with water from the spouted vessel and came back.

'What? Haven't you gone yet?

All of a sudden, Neelakantan fell at Ramunni's feet. He placed his forehead on the white feet that smelled faintly of the rubber tyre sandals that Ramunni habitually wore.

'Hey, che, what are you doing, Neelakantan?'

Meethaledath Ramunni pulled back his feet in haste. Neelakantan's behaviour had upset him. He thought of something and went inside. He took out his money box, placed it before himself and made some calculations. After that he came out again with five hundred rupees.

'This is all I have.'

Neelakantan's eyes shone. He took the money, counted it and put it in the fold of his mundu. However much Ramunni insisted, he did not take back the gold he had brought. Ramunni did not know what to do. He felt insulted. His face got redder as he thought of Neelakantan and the peculiar situation that he had put him in. Finally, he arrived at a decision. In the evening, when he went for a walk, he would return the gold to Neelakantan's wife, Savitri. Neelakantan had taken a lot of money from him and had not returned any of it. He might not return this five hundred too. Still, he could not take the pledge of an ornament and lend money. The Meethaledath family had not descended to that level.

Ramunni put the small bundle in his money box and locked it. No, the Meethaledath family could not descend to such a low level. His ancestors would not forgive him.

He took a bath, changed into a fresh mundu and went to his oil mill. The oil mill was in the old primary school, a building that belonged to the Meethaledath family. When the school shifted to its own building, Ramunni had shifted the oil mill there. The moistness of oil lingered in the compound wall of the mill and the panchayat lamp post outside. Bullock carts that had brought copra to the mill stood in a line outside the building. Ramunni saw a small boy grab a piece of copra and move away.

'Here boy, stop…'

The boy stood holding his hand behind his back, looking at Ramunni with fear in his eyes. All the children of the village feared him because of his high birth and great wealth.

'What's in your hand?'

The boy stood still, rendered speechless by fear.

'Come here.'

The boy did not move. His heart beat fast like the heart of a frightened dove. Ramunni picked up two big pieces of copra and put them in the boy's hands. He felt like laughing when he saw the startled expression in the boy's eyes.

'What's your name?'

'Balagopalan.'

He ran away as fast as he could, holding the copra pieces.

Meethaledath Ramunni went around the mill for a while. The coconut cake that was left over after the oil was extracted lay in a hillock in the front yard. Crows cackled as they flew over it. As the day dawned, all the crows in the area would fly to the surroundings of the mill. Ramunni could feel the moistness of the oil on his face when he stood there for a while. He felt uncomfortable breathing in the oil-heavy air. He never stayed long in the mill because of that. He flagged down a horse cart that was going past and went back to his house.

The Meethaledath family were copra merchants by tradition.

'You don't make the kind of profit you used to in the old days, Achu Master. The coconut trees are also getting diseases like human beings. And copra is going at a low price…'

Achu Master nodded.

'No one can live on copra and coconut in the days to come. You will have to take up smuggling or something like that.'

Both of them laughed at the joke. Ramunni joked and laughed only with Achu Master. Both of them had studied together in the school that had been where the present oil mill was. Meethaledath Ramunni was serious even when he spoke to his wife. He laughed freely with her only in the bathroom. He would massage oil on his body every morning and walk up and down in the yard. Since he was the owner of the oil mill there was never any shortage of oil. It was his wife Sarojini's job to rub away the oil with powdered green gram. When his wife's fingers with their rings touched his armpit, Ramunni would feel ticklish. He would look at his wife and laugh aloud. Sarojini would tickle him again and again to hear that rare laughter. After a while she would also start laughing with him. The servants who would be drawing up water from the well outside would wonder what the husband and wife found to laugh about in the bathroom.

'Where are you going, Ramunni Mooppar?'

'To Neelakantan's house.'

Meethaledath Ramunni held the corner of his mundu with his left hand and walked to Neelakantan's house, with an umbrella in his right hand planting its tip on the ground with each step. He acknowledged the greetings of the people who went past him, lifting his right hand with the umbrella.

The path he was walking down had been just a small lane earlier. Two people could hardly walk abreast. When Ramunni was a child he felt frightened wondering what he would do if the huge cow with curved horns that belonged to Raman Chettiar came from the opposite direction. The thought gave him nightmares on many nights. It was when Ramunni and Achu Master were in the sixth standard that the lane had been widened a little. It was now possible for both Raman Chettiar's big-bellied cow and Kittan who accompanied her to walk side by side through the lane. Still, Ramunni continued to have the nightmare. The only difference was that Chettiar's cow was replaced by the tusker who came at the time of the temple festival. When Ramunni and Achu Master reached the tenth standard, the lane was widened further and became a proper street. The elephants that came for the temple festival, their mahouts and the children who followed the elephants could walk comfortably through the street now.

There, he could see Neelakantan's house now. The woman standing on the veranda and combing her hair after her bath was Neelakantan's wife, Savitri. The people of the village used to wonder how Neelakantan, who was so dark had managed to find such a fair woman as a wife. Even Sarojini, Meethaledath Ramunni's wife, was not half as fair.

Neelakantan was squatting near the well and brushing his teeth. One could hear him hawking and spitting right across the fields. Neelakantan and Savitri had two children. Indira, who sat on the floor that had been smoothed with cow dung and wrote the letters of the alphabet, was the younger one. Balagopalan was the elder one.

He had to hand over the ornament to Savitri and tell her that the Meethaledath family did not believe in taking pledges and lending money. Ramunni walked across the fields. Every now and then his slippers sank into the muddy puddles. Savitri did not see Ramunni who was coming across the fields. Nor did Neelakantan. He finished brushing near the well and left the compound. He must have gone to the stream for a bath. Ramunni touched the fold of his mundu to make sure that the small bundle was still there. Neelakantan had said that it was gold weighing three sovereigns, but Ramunni had not looked at it to see what it was. He had locked up the small bundle exactly as it was given to him in the money box. Now, he suddenly felt curious.Was it a chain? Or bangles? Ramunni opened the bundle and took out the ornament. It was a golden girdle, not too broad, carved intricately. He wrapped it up and put it in the fold of his mundu again. He once again picked up the corner of his mundu, planted the umbrella in the soil and appeared in the yard, climbing the stone steps cut into the wall. Seeing Meethaledath Ramunni all of a sudden, Savitri was startled. Her hand, raised to comb her hair, stayed still for a moment.

'Isn't Neelakantan here?'

Neelakantan had gone towards the stream right before his eyes. Ramunni did not know why he asked her such a stupid question. Savitri wiped the bench with the edge of the mundu she was wearing and asked him to sit. He was amused by her startled expression and her nervousness. Her cheeks were so fair…her hair was so dark…

Oh god, why was Meethaledath Ramunni looking at her so peculiarly, Savitri wondered nervously.

'Why are your neck and arms bare?' Ramunni asked. 'Has he taken everything and pledged them?'

Savitri was standing with her head bent. Her face fell. Ramunni guessed that the girdle that he carried in the fold of his mundu was the one she wore round her waist all the time.

'He took your girdle and pledged that as well, did he?'

A long sigh rose from her. When her father had sent her to Neelakantan he had given her ornaments weighing about fifteen sovereigns. Neelakantan had wasted all of it.

'If nothing else, why don't you buy a few glass bangles and wear them?'

Savitri who was standing with her bare arms on the door post let out another long sigh.

They could see Neelakantan bathing in the water that flowed into the stream from the fields.

'I'm leaving. Have to go to the mill. Some work at the Panchayat office too. When Neelakantan gets back, tell him Meethaledath Ramunni had come.'

'Indira's father will come back soon.'

If Meethaledath Ramunni wanted to see Neelakantan, he only had to send someone over. He didn't need to walk all this distance. Savitri guessed that he had come about some important matter. Her nervousness increased with the thought.

Standing on the veranda, she could see Neelakantan lie half immersed in the water like a black buffalo. Ramunni picked up the corner of the mundu in his left hand. That meant he was about to leave. Savitri hesitated. She could not stop him from going. She couldn't ask him why he had come. She stood there unable to decide what to do.

Ramunni made sure that the ornament was safely in the fold of his mundu and lifted the corner he had in his hand. He started walking, planting the umbrella in the soil at each step. He visited Achu Master at his house on the way. Ramunni felt as if something was amiss if he did not meet Achu Master at least two or three times in a day. When he reached home after drinking the water of a tender coconut from the best tree, he found Neelakantan waiting for him.

'If you'd just sent someone, I would have come,' Neelakantan muttered, appearing guilty about Ramunni's visit.

'Never mind. I just stepped into your house on the way to Achu Master's house. There was no special reason.'

Had Ramunni forgotten that Achu Master's house came before Neelakantan's?

'You can go, Neelakantan. As for the money, there's no hurry about it. Give it back when you can.'

Neelakantan did not understand anything. He felt angry with Savitri who had dragged him out of the stream and sent him here.

'No hurry at all,' Meethaledath Ramunni repeated.

Two

The bedroom upstairs was rather dark. So, Ramunni moved to the window and opened the bundle again. His thick fingers caressed the golden girdle. The gold was so cool. He stood there for some time, just looking at it. He would send someone to call Neelakantan and return the ornament. This girdle was not meant to lie in his cash box. Let it go back to where it belonged, round Savitri's waist.

When he heard Sarojini's footsteps on the stairs, he put the bundle back into the fold of his mundu, picked up a fan, and stood near the window fanning himself.

'Why did you come upstairs in this heat?' Sarojini came close, put her hand affectionately on her husband's shoulder and asked.

'Why did that Neelakantan come again? Do you have any idea how much cash you have given him already? Don't give him another paisa,' she scolded her husband. He gave away anything anyone asked for. If he kept giving away money to anyone who came…The income of the family was going down. The tharavad was declining.

'Sarojini, don't you know that if you give one, god returns it as two?'

There was no man who was as generous as Meethaledath Ramunni. Even the false tooth in Achu Master's mouth had been bought with the money provided by Ramunni. Achu Master who had seven children was always in need of money. But he was too proud to go around the place and borrow from anyone like that Neelakantan. If Ramunni had given his friend money now and then it was not because Achu Master had asked him. He had seen his friend's need and given him freely. Life was a sea without a shore to Achu Master. He had got only the eldest of his four daughters married so far. As the two friends sat on the culvert in the evening, enjoying the breeze, Ramunni would tell Achu Master, 'Achu, you don't have to worry as long as I'm alive.Don't waste time thinking about how things will work out. By god's grace the Meethaledath family has enough wealth even now to marry off thirty girls, why only three.'

Ramunni and his wife came down the wooden stairs. It was time for him to go for his walk.

Achu Master would be waiting at the culvert.

'Did you return Neelakantan's gold?' He enquired.

Ramunni hesitated for a moment, 'Yes, I returned it…'

It was probably the first time in their forty years of acquaintance that Ramunni had lied to Achu Master.

'My dear Ramunni, you are too innocent for this life. Do you imagine that you'll get back the money from that Neelakantan now? You can bid your money goodbye.'

'Never mind. I've given so much to so many people like this.'

'That's what I said, you are too innocent to live in this world.'

Achu Master smiled, showing the denture. His teeth shone even at this age due to the daily brushing with burnt rice husk. The false tooth with its dull colour stood out from the natural teeth. He had not lost that tooth from decay. He'd slipped and fallen in his front yard and lost a tooth.

When the 7:30 local train passed under the overbridge, the friends started walking home.

As soon as he reached home, Ramunni washed his face, hands and feet with lukewarm water and went straight upstairs. Two workers from the mill and Chappan Nair who leased the coconut trees were waiting for him. Ramunni pretended not to have seen them and went upstairs to his bedroom. Chappan Nair asked himself what had happened to Meethaledath Ramunni. He had come with the accounts and the money for the coconuts plucked. After waiting for some time, he went away. If Meethaledath Ramunni did not have the time to receive the money, well, Thattinpurath Chappan Nair did not have the time to give the money either. But the workers, Raman and Pokkan, did not leave like Chappan Nair. They had come for their wages and were worried that the toddy shop would close very soon. Raman was a tall man and Pokkan was short unlike his name which meant 'tall man'.When their legs ached from standing, they squatted in the yard.

Sarojini came and stood near the bottom of the stairs. Looking up she said in a loud voice, 'Raman and Pokkan have been waiting for a long time.Why don't you give them whatever you have to and send them away?'

Ramunni started at the sound of his wife's voice and hid the girdle in the fold of his mundu. He came down like a sleepwalker and gave Raman and Pokkan their wages. They bowed and headed straight to the toddy shop.

'What were you doing upstairs? Chappan Nair waited for a long time and went away.'

'Let him go,' Meethaledath Ramunni said in a feeble voice to no one in particular.

'Oh god! What's happened to you?' Sarojini looked at her husband carefully. He seemed lost in a world of his own. She knew that he did not drink but smelled his mouth to make sure. His mouth held the smell of perfumed areca nut.

'If you're not well, have your gruel early and go to sleep.'

Looking around to make sure that no one was watching them, Sarojini took her husband's hand and caressed it. That caress did not give him any relief. On the other hand, it made him feel worse.

Ramunni drank his gruel hurriedly. And then went equally hurriedly to the bedroom upstairs. Once there, he shut the door of the room and bolted it so that no one would trouble him.

After that day, he always carried Savitri's girdle with him everywhere. As he walked to the mill, he would look around, make sure that there was no one about and take it out of the fold of his mundu. Sometimes, he would run his fingers over it and caress it. When he was at home, he would go upstairs every now and then. One day his wife followed him. He did not realize that she was coming. As soon as he reached his bedroom, he took out the girdle and sat looking at it. It was only when he heard footsteps on the boards just beyond the door that he realized that Sarojini was close by. He hid the girdle in the fold of his mundu with tiger-like quickness.

'What are you doing, sitting here alone?' His wife came and stood near him. He realized that she had not seen the girdle through the grace of god. He heaved a sigh of relief.

Sarojini did not know that Neelakantan had pledged Savitri's girdle. All she knew was that he had given three sovereigns of gold as pledge. She had not displayed even the usual feminine curiosity and asked whether the ornament was a chain or bangles. She did not interfere in her husband's affairs usually. She did not know how much oil was milled or how many people worked in the oil mill. Once in a while when she saw him giving away something, she would say that his generosity was getting to be a little too much. That was all.

'Let me lie down for a while, Sarojini. I'm feeling so tired...'

The bed groaned when Ramunni lay down. It was around a hundred years old. Ramunni's mother had given birth to him lying on this bed. Sarojini had conceived his four children lying on this bed. He held Savitri's girdle close to his chest like a child sucking its fingers and curled up. That night he dreamt of Savitri's fair waist, wearing that girdle made of old gold.

Ramunni woke up very disturbed. He sent back the kavuthiyyan, who had come to give him a shave as always. He paced the yard for a long time. He didn't bathe. Nor did he go to the mill.

'What's wrong with you? I've been seeing this for the past two days. You aren't your usual self. What are you so preoccupied with? Can't you tell me, whatever it is? Am I some outsider? I want to know what it is that you have on your mind.'

Sarojini had never spoken like that to her husband. This was the first time.

'My dear Sarojini, what secret do I have that you don't know?' Meethaledath Ramunni looked at his wife and smiled. He also caressed her buttocks making sure that no one else was looking. The answer and the gesture made her happy. She went in. She always had work in the kitchen.

Ramunni thought only of the dream he had had the previous night as he walked and went about his usual routine. The gold girdle, dulled with use, that encircled a fair waist.

Oh god! What am I doing? I'm fifty years old. I have a wife and four children. And still, I dream of the waist of someone else's wife. Thinking that, he walked to Neelakantan's house. As usual, he walked proudly, holding the corner of his mundu, and planting the tip of his umbrella on the ground with each step.

Achu Master who sat in front of his house waved and shouted out something. Ramunni did not see or hear anything.

Seeing Ramunni in the front yard again, Savitri was surprised. Neelakantan was not there. He did not have any permanent job and came and went as he pleased. Now that it was summer, his favourite occupation was to lie immersed in the stream. One day, lying in the water like that, he had fallen asleep. A lot of water got into his eyes and nose. He had swallowed some too. On hearing that story, Savitri had laughed the whole day.

'Is Neelakantan here?'

'No.' She stood half-hidden by the door.

Ramunni hesitated, not knowing what to say after that. He could see a portion of her hips as she stood behind the door. There was only a small difference between the hips he had seen in his dream and the hips he saw now. The hips in his dream were not covered by any cloth.

'Has he gone to the stream to bathe?'

'No.'

'When he comes back, tell him I asked for him.'

Savitri came out from behind the door. Her eyes looked as though they had been outlined with oil.

'Ramunni Mooppar, you must be patient for some more time. We'll return all the money soon.'

Ramunni was so happy to hear her speak that he could hardly bear it. Hiding his feelings and making his voice heavy, he said, 'Savitri, the Meethaledath family now only has a name. I too have four children to bring up.'

Savitri's face fell. There was nothing more in the house to sell or pledge. Her husband had taken the last thing left from round her waist while she was asleep. When she caught sight of her bare waist as she stood behind the overgrown grass in the stream and bathed, she would sigh. Only the children were left to pledge or sell. She wouldn't be surprised if one day Neelakantan took Indira and Balagopalan and pledged them too...

As she stood there thinking of all that, he stood and looked at her hips.

Three

When Neelakantan reached home in the evening, he found Savitri with her eyes filled with tears.

'Meethaledath Ramunni Mooppar had come again today.'

'For the money?'

'Why else would he come?'

'I'll pay off all the debts before I die.'

He sat on the veranda with a feeling of hatred for the whole world. His shirt was soaked in sweat. He took it off and threw it on to the clothesline.

'Why are you still whimpering?'

'I want my girdle.'

'Are you a child now to go around wearing a girdle?'

'Sell anything you like. I want my girdle back.'

'You'll drive me mad one of these days.'

With that he picked up his towel and went to the stream.

Savitri did not give him any peace after that. She threatened that she would go to her home and take Indira and Balagopalan along. And so, Neelakantan came to see Ramunni once again. Ramunni was in the bedroom at that time. The door was shut tight. When he heard that Neelakantan had come, he came down.

'What is it, Neelakantan? Do you want more money?'

Neelakantan wondered if Ramunni was making fun of him.

'Don't hesitate. Tell me.'

'Savitri is not giving me any peace...'

'Why's that?'

'She says she wants her girdle.'

When he heard that, Ramunni grew pale. He was afraid that Sarojini would hear what Neelakantan was saying. As it is, she hated the sight of him. Ramunni got out into the yard. He took Neelakantan with him and walked outside. The sun was burning hot overhead. They stood behind the wall, where Sarojini could not see him. The moss on the wall had dried up in the heat and lay like ashes here and there.

'If you have anything to tell me, I'll come to your place. You needn't come here.'

Ramunni's words and peculiar behaviour upset Neelakantan. Meethaledath Ramunni would come to see the permanently jobless Neelakantan in his home! What had happened to Ramunni Mooppar?

'Go now! I'll come to your place when I go to the mill in the evening. You can tell me whatever you want to then.'

Neelakantan did not say anything. He did not know what to think. Ramunni took out a ten-rupee note from his pocket and gave it to Neelakantan, saying, 'Go and have some tea.'

When Neelakantan left, a long sigh rose from Ramunni.

He kept his word. On his way back from the mill he went to Neelakantan's house. Savitri was full of wonder on seeing Meethaledath Ramunni again. 'There's Ramunni Mooppar again,' she said. Neelakantan tightened the mundu that had become loose around his waist and came to the veranda. Ramunni planted his umbrella and stepped on to the veranda. He sat on the bench without being invited.

'You can tell me whatever you want to say.'

He sat there, willing to listen. But Neelakantan did not say anything. He had gone to Meethaledath in the morning because Savitri had insisted.

'What Neelakantan, don't you have anything to say?'

'No.'

'Then why did you come to my house early in the morning, and start saying this and that in front of everyone?'

'Ramunni Mooppar, you must give that girdle back to me.'

'You pledged it with me.'

'I'll return the money soon.'

'I'm not in a hurry, Neelakantan.'

Neelakantan did not know what more to say. When he had offered the girdle as a pledge, Ramunni had tried to refuse the pledge. He, Neelakantan, had insisted that he take it.

There was a movement at the door. Ramunni looked towards the door. He could see Savitri's hair and a part of her hips behind the door. His heart beat faster.

'Neelakantan, don't ask me for the girdle. I'll give you anything else.' Ramunni spoke in a pleading voice. 'It's three sovereigns, isn't it? I'll give you the money for five sovereigns. Will that do?'

Neelakantan's eyes shone. He felt sure that Ramunni had lost the girdle. That was good. How could he garner five hundred rupees to get it back when he did not even have a job? Ramunni did not have to give him the price of five sovereigns. He only had to give him the price of three and the cost of making the ornament. Neelakantan could then return his five hundred rupees and keep what remained. He had averted a big problem.

'What? Are you agreeable?'

Neelakantan nodded to say yes.

'I'll bring the money tomorrow at this time.'

Neelakantan nodded again.

As he went down the steps, the corner of his mundu in one hand and the tip of the umbrella placed on the ground, with each step, Ramunni was shouting mentally with joy. The joy of having conquered a whole world. He stood on the raised portion of the fields and took out the girdle from the fold of his mundu and gazed at it to his heart's content. He rubbed it against both his cheeks and kissed it.

Four

Work at the oil mill went on as usual. The copra came by bullock carts. Carts with tins of oil stacked in them went to the town. Meethaledath Ramunni's empire seemed to have an endless supply of coconuts that would not finish however long the mills worked. The remaining coconuts were taken by Chappan Nair on lease. Ramunni made Neelakantan his manager. He could take as many coconuts and as much oil as he wanted. When Neelakantan came out of the stream after a bath, a film of coconut oil lay on the water. It looked as though Balagopalan's and Indira's faces dripped with oil.

'You don't have to put such a lot on your head and face just because it is free,' Achu Master teased him.

There was a reason for Achu Master's comment. He did not understand why Ramunni needed to make Neelakantan his manager. Neelakantan was one of those people who could not stick to any job for long. Wasn't that why he had been without a proper job all these years, even after he fathered two children? Besides, Ramunni did not need a manager. He had plenty of dependants to look after his property and the oil mill.

'How long can he go around like this? After all, there are two children to be considered,' said Ramunni when asked.

The kitchen fire burned everyday in Neelakantan's house. Now that they had curry with their rice and bathed with coconut oil, the children glowed.

Once, while Neelakantan was standing in the mill supervising the loading of the coconut cake into the carts, Ramunni got into his bullock cart and went to Neelakantan's house. He stopped the cart at the edge of the fields and walked to the house.

'Isn't anyone here?'

'Mother's bathing.'

'Where, son?'

'There,' Balagopalan pointed to the stream in the distance.

There were reeds growing to the height of a man there. Indira was sitting in the mud in the yard and making sand houses with coconut shells. Ramunni looked at the reeds. Beyond the reeds lay the stream. The water was clearer there. Small fish would be playing at the bottom of the stream, among the stems of the reeds.

'You're going, Ramunni Mooppar?'

'Got some work, son.'

He took out two coins of four annas each and gave them to Balagopalan and Indira and asked, 'How much is this?'

'Four annas.'

'Can you get orange sweets for this?'

'Lots and lots.'

'No, my mother will beat me,' Balagopalan put down the money. As soon as she saw that, Indira also dropped the coin in the mud.

'Your mother won't beat you. Just tell her that Ramunni Mooppar gave it to you.'

The children picked up the coins doubtfully.

Ramunni got out hastily. His bullock cart stood at a distance at the edge of the field. The bullock was chewing the cud after a meal of straw and water in the morning. There was foam between its big teeth. Cowdung was scattered between its hind legs.

There, Meethaledath Ramunni hid among the reeds that grew taller than him. His feet, in their tyre slippers, sank into the slush. He saw the hips which held the mark of the girdle, now in the fold of his mundu, as though in a dream. He stood there in the coolness of the green grass and the water as though turned into a statue. Ramunni did not notice the time pass.

Five

Achu Master felt that there was something odd in Ramunni's behaviour. As he sat on the veranda, he noticed that the barber who had come in the morning to give Ramunni a shave returned without doing his job. Achu Master could see all the comings and goings from his veranda. The only big street in the village passed in front of his house. The bullock carts that took the copra to the mill passed by on that road. The children went to school that way. Ramunni and Achu Master still went for their usual walk every day. But sometimes Ramunni would be sunk in silence. He did not even hear what Achu master said. He was in some other world.

What was that world? Whose was that world? That was what Achu Master did not know.

Sarojini also noticed the gradual change in her husband's behaviour. Earlier, once he came down from his room, he would go up only after his midday meal for a short nap. Nowadays he went up at least ten times a day. Sometimes, he would come down, pause as though he had thought of something and go up again.

'Why don't you stay upstairs permanently? You won't

have to climb those stairs a hundred times then,' she would comment sarcastically.

One day, as her husband went upstairs she followed him silently. He went into the bedroom, shut the door and stood near the window with his back to the door. Sarojini peered through the gaps in the door. She had never interfered in her husband's affairs. She had never doubted him even for a moment. It was not curiosity, but anxiety about her husband's behaviour that prompted her to spy on him. There was light coming from the small window. She saw Ramunni take something from the fold of his mundu, look at it intently and then hold it to his chest and his eyes.Since he was standing with his back to the room, she could not see what it was that he held in his hand. By this time their youngest son came crying, in search of his mother. Ramunni awoke from his reverie at the sound and hid the girdle in his mundu again.

'What business have you both here?' Ramunni got angry. 'You won't let me have any peace.'

'You can kill me and the children. Then you can spend your time in peace, isn't it?'

She picked up her son and wiped his nose. He always had a running nose. His name was Sahadevan. She went downstairs with him. Ramunni sat there wrapped in thought. He did not shave or bathe that day.

He did not go for his walk that evening. Achu Master stood alone on the bridge, looking at the railway line below. A train was coming down the rails, spitting smoke.

Darkness fell quickly that day because it was overcast. Achu Master came back to his house earlier than usual. He saw Ramunni walk towards Neelakantan's house. These constant visits to Neelakantan's house, giving Neelakantan the manager's job – what did all this mean? Oh god...

He said to Sarojini, 'Be careful as far as Ramunni's concerned. Remember that you have children who are very small.'

'I don't understand anything, Achu Master...'

'You'll understand everything in time. Just pay attention to this now.'

'Oh god! What'll I do?' Sarojini's eyes filled with tears.

'Don't worry too much, Sarojini. I just mentioned something that I've been feeling. If you're careful now, you won't have to be sorry later.'

After Achu Master went away, Sarojini stood with Sahadevan at her hip and wiped her eyes. Meethaledath Ramunni had never made his wife cry. He'd given her everything she wanted. Now, a quarter of a century after he had tied the thali round her neck, he was making her cry. From what Achu Master had said, she realized that some other woman had taken over her husband's mind. Who could that cunning woman be to bewitch her husband at fifty years of age? She would find out that very day. She waited for him.

But when Ramunni came in and she saw his unshaven face and wounded eyes, she stood there without saying anything. Her glance fell accidentally on the fold of his mundu. Something glinted there. She had seen him hide something in the fold of the mundu when she approached him many times recently. Her face changed colour. Whatever secret Meethaledath Ramunni held in his heart was hidden in the fold of his mundu too. Sarojini had to know what it was. She moved closer to her husband.

'What's in that fold?'

'Nothing.'

'You've been hiding it all this time. I want to see it today.'

'There's nothing in the fold of my mundu, Sarojini…'

'You're lying to me, after twenty-five years of living together?'

He looked pathetically at his wife's face.

'It's the gold pledged by Neelakantan.'

'Why can't I see Neelakantan's gold?'

'You needn't see it, Sarojini.'

He started going up the stairs. She followed him.

'I want to know one way or the other today…'

'What do you want to know?'

'Whether it's to be me or her.'

Ramunni was stunned. 'What are you rambling on about, Sarojini?'

'You needn't try to hide anything. I know everything. Aren't you ashamed of yourself? You have children who are over twenty! Must you get into such things at this age…'

Ramunni looked pathetically at his wife again. When their eyes met, he turned his face away.

'How can you look at your children's faces?'

She felt more anger than sorrow. She gazed at her husband with the look of a wounded animal. Suddenly she grabbed the gold ornament from the fold of her husband's mundu. He had not expected such a violent attack from his wife. As he stood there shocked, she opened out the girdle.

Her eyes spewed fire, 'How can you be so shameless? To carry the girdle some woman wears round her hips in the fold of your mundu?'

He took back the girdle and held it tightly in his fist.

'Who's she?'

He did not reply. He went back down the stairs and walked out like a sleep-walker. Even his gait had changed. This was not that old proud stride with the corner of the mundu held in one hand and the umbrella planted firmly at each step. He walked uncertainly like a blind drunk. He did not see people who came from the opposite side. He did not hear what people said to him. This was not the old Meethaledath Ramunni.

Six

Achu Master saw Ramunni walking on the street at a distance as he sat on his veranda. Sitting there, he could recognize anyone coming from any distance. His eyes were very sharp. He applied some ayurvedic eyedrops twice a day. He had been doing so for years and years. He should have good eyesight to be able to read letters even at the age of ninety. That was his prayer to god every day.

He saw Ramunni stop suddenly as he walked down the street. He stood like a statue, holding something before his face. There were fields on either side of the street. There was not even a tree to offer shade from the hot sun. After a little while, Ramunni started walking again. But when he reached the turning to the Panchayat, he turned into a statue again. Holding something before his eyes, he stood there motionless for a while.

Achu Master went alone for walks these days. Ramunni did not join him. When the boy at the ferry brought him his morning newspaper, Achu Master would go as usual to Meethaledath and sit in the gatehouse and read it aloud, but Ramunni would not pay any attention. His mind would be elsewhere. Ramunni did not give clear replies to Achu

Master's questions. Words and syllables came out broken. Ramunni had reached such a state that he could not utter even one full sentence clearly. Achu Master had also noticed that very often Ramunni spoke disconnectedly. Now, it was as though the change in his mind had affected his body as well. His face, which had a golden glow earlier, now had dark patches here and there. Instead of walking proudly with his head held high and shoulders back, he now slouched like a hunchback, planting the tip of the umbrella on the ground with each step.

Meethaledath Ramunni continued walking till he reached Achu Master's house. He did not see his friend who stood in front of the house. He continued to walk as though he had lost all sense of his surroundings. Achu Master got out of his compound and followed Ramunni as he walked along the street. When he passed the astrologer's house and reached the lamp post put up by the Panchayat, Ramunni's legs stopped. He took out the girdle from the fold of his mundu, held it before his face and stood there with his gaze fixed on it as though he had been changed into a statue of stone. He did not see Achu Master who had stopped near him.

'Ramunni, what's that in your hand?'

Ramunni did not move even then. He did not see Achu Master. Nor did he hear what he said.

After a little while, Ramunni placed the girdle in the fold of his mundu and started walking again. Achu Master did not follow him. He stood under the Panchayat lamp post and watched Ramunni walk towards the paddy fields. After you crossed the fields and walked by the stream, you reached Neelakantan's house.

Ramunni had been his friend since childhood. They were classmates and had grown up together. They had no secrets from each other. Though they were of the same age, Achu Master was more worldly-wise and balanced. That is why Ramunni sought his advice on all matters. When the villagers started noticing Ramunni's peculiar behaviour, they went to Achu Master first. Ramunni was moving towards some big danger, Achu Master told himself as he stood under the lamp post. He had to rescue Ramunni from this danger at whatever cost. That was his duty.

Achu Master folded up his mundu, walked straight, turned to the right and got down into the field behind his friend. When he reached the side of the stream, he saw Ramunni enter the thicket of grass in the distance. What was Ramunni doing there where all sorts of rodents and snakes lived? Everything Ramunni did these days surprised Achu Master.

One of Ramunni's rubber sandals lay submerged and abandoned at the place where the grass started. Achu Master had no problem recognising the slippers. Only Meethaledath Ramunni wore slippers in that village. Achu Master parted the grass and entered the thicket. Ramunni sat on the side of the stream behind the grass as though he were waiting for someone. Though Achu Master made a lot of noise as he stepped through the water, Ramunni sat oblivious to it. He was sitting there motionless, staring at the clear water of the stream. Crushed leaves floated around, left behind after the juice was used to wash hair, and an empty bottle that had held oil lay on a stone. The damp smell of the long soap used by the village women to wash clothes lingered in the air. What reason did Meethaledath Ramunni have to come and sit here?

Achu Master suddenly became conscious of his surroundings. He was a teacher who taught the alphabet to the children of the village. What if someone saw him hiding among the thick grass at the place where women bathed? Achu Master shuddered. He turned around and walked back out of the grass without making a sound. He looked around to make sure that he had not been seen by anyone. He returned home, relieved. Leaving behind Meethaledath Ramunni there…

After a couple of days, Ramunni's wife Sarojini came to see Achu Master. She came with eyes reddened by weeping. Achu Master listened patiently to everything she said. When he heard that Ramunni was carrying a girdle worn by some woman round her hips in the fold of his mundu, he felt ashamed of him. He could not even look Sarojini in the face.

'That female who's trying to make orphans of my children and throw me out of my house, I'll stab her in the eyes.'

'Be calm, Sarojini, we'll find a solution to this.

'Achu Master, I want to know who she is…'

'We'll find out.'

Cursing some more, and weeping some more, she returned home. Achu Master now understood everything. That girdle was the curse that was gripping Ramunni. He also knew whose girdle it was.

He first thought of telling Neelakantan about it. But would he be able to bear the news? It was true that Ramunni had helped him a lot. He'd made him his manager. It was Neelakantan who supervised the working of the oil mill now. But still, would Neelakantan tolerate this? That some other man carried the girdle that had been round his wife's hips in the fold of his mundu. That he was obsessed with it. Not just Neelakantan, no man would be able to bear this and stand around with folded hands. No, it was better that Neelakantan did not know anything about this for now.

But he went the same day to speak to Savitri. When she saw Achu Master come up the steps cut out of sandstone, Savitri wondered what was happening. Recently, the most important people of the village were coming to her house. Achu Master, who had never looked at her, who had never even asked, 'How are you, Savitri?' for politeness's sake when he saw her on the road, was standing hesitantly in her front yard.

'Is Neelakantan here?'

'No, he's at the oil mill.'

Achu Master was relieved. If Neelakantan had been there he would have had to go back without saying what he had come to say.

'You can see him if you go to the mill.'

'I didn't come here to see Neelakantan; I came to see you.'

Savitri looked surprised. She wiped her wet hands on the edge of her mundu. When he caught sight of her white midriff between the blouse and the mundu, Achu Master turned his face away. She wore black glass bangles on both arms. Achu Master took out some money form the pocket of his shirt. A lot of tens and fives and twos, all dirty and crumpled.

'Here, this is five hundred rupees.'

'What's it for?'

'You take this.'

Though she did not understand anything, Savitri took the money. Who wouldn't take money when it was held out?

'Take this, pay off your debt and get back your girdle.'

'The girdle was sold to Ramunni Mooppar. He gave us the price of the gold and the making charge of the goldsmith.'

Achu Master did not know that. He scratched his head. He no longer knew what was happening in Ramunni's life. He was a stranger to him now...

'Why aren't you saying anything, Achu Master?'

'What can I say, Savitri?'

'Why did you tell me to get back the girdle?'

Achu Master sat there on the veranda with his head bent.

'Here's your money...'

He took the money and put it in his pocket. Savitri could not understand anything... Why had Achu Master come with the money? Why did he want her girdle? Meethaledath Ramunni had walked up those stone steps a number of times. It was after that he had gone crazy. Achu Master who had never paid any attention to her had also come here today. Would Achu Master also go crazy like Ramunni? Savitri looked at him carefully...

'Savitri...' Achu Master's voice seemed to come from somewhere very distant.

'Meethaledath Ramunni is from the most aristocratic family in this place. Ramunni has never behaved in any way below his dignity. And now, look at Ramunni. He doesn't eat, he doesn't sleep. He doesn't bathe, he doesn't change his clothes. He walks around like a mad man. Two days back someone saw Ramunni in the toddy shop. He was sitting with the scavengers and drinking toddy...'

Savitri's face fell. She asked, 'Why are you telling me all this?'

'Who can I say all this to, but you? You are the reason for all this. You and that girdle of yours.'

Savitri's eyes opened wide. She had also heard that something was wrong with Meethaledath Ramunni. Neelakantan himself had told her about it. But how could she be the reason for Ramunni's bad times?

'As long as your girdle is in the fold of Ramunni's mundu, he will not escape this curse. Savitri, I'll touch your feet. Go and get it back...'

She still did not understand anything. And so, Achu Master had to explain everything. She sat there, stunned by what she heard.

Seven

There was rain somewhere far off and the water of the stream was muddied and reddened. Small fish swam in the muddied water and rubbed against Savitri's ankles. As she bent to immerse herself in the water and then rose again, the ripples reached the roots of the grass and vanished. She could see two butterflies flying around among the stalks of the grass. They had been flying around there even when she entered the stream. She went down into the water again and again and swam around a little. Savitri could swim very well. When she had been a small child, her father had taken her to the temple pond and taught her to swim. She had lain on her father's hairy hands extended before him and paddled her feet and steered with her hands till she learnt how to swim.

There was a separate flight of steps leading to the pond for the women who came to bathe there. When she was in the third standard something unfortunate happened. When she reached home after her bath, the girdle was not around her hips. Her mother cried and ran to the pond. The girdle could not be found anywhere. Her mother came back crying. As soon as her father came for lunch, her mother told him and he went immediately to the steps of the pond. The women who had been bathing there moved here and there and hid themselves as well as they could. As they stood and watched, her father vanished into the water near the steps. He did not come up for many minutes. The hearts of the women beat harder in unison. Savitri was terrified. As everyone watched anxiously, fearfully, her father came up out of the water, golden girdle in hand.

She put out her hand and took the girdle from him, and tied it around her slim waist. 'I'll never lose this girdle again,' she said to herself with tears in her eyes.

As she grew up and started menstruating, the girdle became tight around her waist, leaving its mark. Still, she did not take it off. As her waist became broader, one day the girdle broke.It fell through her skirt, rubbing against her legs. She cried, looking at the broken girdle in her hands.

'Why are you crying, Savitri?' her mother asked. She consoled her, 'We'll give it to the goldsmith and get it mended.'

When her father came home that day, her mother told him about the girdle being broken.

'Never mind. I'll ask the goldsmith to come in the evening.'

The goldsmith came in the evening and took away the girdle. He added three quarters of a sovereign to the gold and remade the girdle. It took him four days to complete the work. The four days she spent without the girdle round her hips, Savitri was sad and lost. It was as if she had forgotten something somewhere... as if she had lost something...

'This won't break even if an elephant tries to break it,' the goldsmith said as he handed over the girdle to Savitri. 'Go and wear it.'

'He's done a good job,' said her mother turning it this way and that after the goldsmith left. 'Though he's drunk most of the time, he knows his work.'

She ran to her room, shut the door and wore the girdle round her waist.

She had never taken it off after that. After her marriage, after two children were born, Neelakantan had taken it from her by guile. That was how it had reached the fold of Meethaledath Ramunni's mundu.

She could bear to be away from her children. But she couldn't bear to be without her girdle. She couldn't sleep. Even if she slept, she would wake in the middle of the night and search for the girdle. It was not an ornament, but a part of her body like her eyes or her nose. When she had realized that Neelakantan had taken it away from her waist while she was sleeping, she had cried and cried.

She stood chest-deep in water and thought of all sorts of things... The thicket of grass and the stream were golden in the sunlight. She immersed herself in the water and stood up straight again. Water flowed like rivulets from her hair and shoulders and breasts.

The butterflies were still playing among the grass. She became a small child again and walked through the water silently to extend her hands to the butterflies. She wanted to hold those butterflies and caress them. There was mud in the water around the grass. Her feet got sucked in the mud. The butterflies appeared and disappeared into the dense green of the grass. She followed the butterflies through the water with the stubbornness of a small child.

When she saw two thin hands come through the grass

towards her with the girdle held open in them, she stood motionless.

Ramunni tied the golden girdle around Savitri's waist with trembling hands. Long ago, when he had tied the thali round Sarojini's neck, his hands had trembled the same way.

The Naked Lord

One

There was a lord in Kallissery. His name was Kunhikrishnan Thampuran. He was richer than god and handsomer too. He was god incarnate to the people of Kallissery. The women would be dazzled at the sight of him. The men would take off their turbans and tie them round their waist. The lord was against all newfangled things. When he saw the youngest son of the schoolmaster walking along in long pants he immediately ordered the coachman to stop the judka (a horse-driven cart).

'Where do you come from? England?'

'God, no, I am the schoolmaster's son.'

'Then go around like the schoolmaster's son. If I see you in these long pants I'll break your legs for you.'

The boy was afraid. He had the intelligence to understand that though Kallissery had been created by god, it was ruled by its Thampuran.

The lord travelled by judka, not because he could not afford to buy a jeep or a car. He believed that motor vehicles were newfangled things. A motor car did not have the aristocracy of the judka. Aristocracy and respectability mattered most to him. He often said that it was better to hang oneself than to live in disgrace. So people lived lives of respectability and decorum. Even when no fires burned in their kitchens, they did not borrow. Even when family members had been quarrelling bitterly at home, when they went out, they laughed and joked. There was hardly any theft or robbery in the place. Even if something was lost from a house they did not mention it in public. They felt it was a disgrace to let others know that there was a thief in Kallissery. The honour of the women had to be protected even at the cost of lives. That too was the order of the lord.

'What is it, Govindan?'

The Thampuran stood on the front veranda after his bath and a breakfast of milky gruel. He wore a single dhoti around his golden stomach and carried a fan in his hand. Some ten or fifteen people stood in the front yard with their hands folded.This was routine. Even when he had to stay in bed due to a cold or something else, the Thampuran would give this morning audience to the people.

'Dechu delivered.'

'Very good, very good, how many does that make?'

'This is the sixth.'

'You may have one more. Stop at seven.'

The audience lasted till 9 o'clock. The lord gave advice and instruction to the people. After that he stepped out for a round of the village with his escort to supervise the sowing and the reaping. He sat in the judka and travelled through the market. Looked around to see whether any cheeky boys were wandering around in long pants.

When he saw the policeman sitting in front of the small shop and chewing pan his face grew red.

'What are you doing here?'

'I came to enquire about a sheep that was stolen.'

'Take off your cap and hold it in your hand when you talk to me.'

The policeman took off his cap and held it under his arm.

'Whose sheep is it that is lost?'

'Kunhiraman Master's.'

Master was an outsider who lived across the river. The lord grew angrier.

'No one in Kallissery has been reduced to such straits that they have to cross the river and steal Kunhiraman Master's sheep. Do you understand?'

The policeman nodded.

'Then start walking. There is a boat at the landing. Your cap should not be seen here again.'

The policeman escaped with his cap under his arm.

The lord could not bear the sight or sound of the government or its agencies of law. When he saw the pictures of ministers in newspapers wearing the Gandhi cap and showing all their teeth, he could hardly control himself. He had informed the government that they did not need an election in Kallissery. But the government did not agree.

'All right, I'll show you,' said the lord.

Elections came. The opposing candidate was Raman Chetty who sold coarse towels. He was an outsider. People from across the river campaigned for Raman Chetty. He got four votes. Even Chetty's wife voted for the lord. The lord got him evicted from the shop and ordered that no one should buy towels from him. His children cried of hunger in the house.

'Forgive me.'

'You showed such impudence that you don't deserve to be forgiven!'

'The people from the other side of the river misled me.'

Chetty fell at the Thampuran's feet and held them tight. He was tall and big. And his hands were rough.

'Your wife voted for me. So I forgive you.' The Thampuran returned the key of the shop to Chetty and he went on with his sale of towels.

Chetty came from the colony of weavers across the river and settled here. He was actually not a weaver, but an oil-miller.

His body got its strength and grace from eating oil-cakes. He learnt weaving from the colony of weavers across the river. He came to Kallissery with a first-class woman. A woman with a honey-coloured body and dark black hair. It was an elopement.

'What is your woman's name?'

'Lakshmi.'

'She does not look like a miller-woman.'

'She is from the weavers' community.'

'All right, you can go,' said the Thampuran. He had seen the miller-women in town. During the Onam season, when he went to the town with a cartful of bananas he had seen the miller-women who came to sell oil and curds. The folds of fat on those women hurt the exceptional, beauty-conscious eyes of the lord. But the figures of the weaver-women were always a source of pleasure to his eyes.

'Chetty, look after your Lakshmi well. Someone might steal her away.'

In reply Chetty pulled out a dagger from his waist. The lord got a shock. He had not known that the miller was carrying such a weapon.

'This is Kallissery. One does not need to carry knives and daggers here. I will not permit any woman to be insulted.'

Chetty put the dagger back in his waistband.

The Thampuran had offered complete protection to women in his election manifesto. Wasn't that why even Lakshmi had voted for him? In Kallissery, any woman could bathe in the river at any time of the day. Even if she bathed in the nude, not a soul would dare peep. The lord would go to the bathing ghat and ask.

'Does anyone trouble you?'

'No, Thampuran.'

'Tell me if you are troubled by anyone. I'll arrange for a watchman here.'

'Oh no, it is not necessary.'

The Thampuran always spoke facing away from the river.

'Will he lose his eyesight if he looks at us once?' The women asked each other after the lord left.

'The sanctity of its women is the sanctity of the land. If one woman is insulted here, you can rest assured that Kallissery has been insulted.'

The lord was a man who valued his words. His deeds followed his words. The men would go to the town for all sorts of business. The lord would keep an eye on their women. The men knew that they did not have to worry about the chastity of their women as long as the lord was around.

They did not return to Kallissery even when they had finished their business. They wandered around the town and watched movies in the big cinema theatre. They winked at the miller-women who sold oil in the market and ate biryani at the Muslim hotels.

The lord wished to make Kallissery a model village before he died. Children who grew up good and obedient. Women who were chaste. Merchants who could be trusted. No hoarding or black marketing. Girls who went to the temple daily with wet hair loose, after their morning ablutions. No idle youngsters. Their guardians should give the girls in marriage as soon as they completed their studies. Everyone had to be innoculated. People had to help each other willingly with rice and money during times of scarcity or they should approach the lord. Newfangled things like long pants were not permitted. The shop owners had to sell pure, unadulterated arrack. Elections and zindabads and processions were forbidden. Everyone had to believe in god, and in the lord.

But the lord once made a mistake and he lost his clothes because of that. And he had to hide in the quarry, not to save the good name of other people's women but his own good name.

Two

The hot summer months had started and the land was steaming. The Thampuran could not bear the heat. As the heat increased, the power failures also grew more frequent. He could not accept the logic of that. Should it not be the other way?

Electricity had come to Kallissery recently. But all, including the lord, had fallen under its magic spell. He became restless if there was a power failure for half an hour and the fan stopped rotating. This was exactly what happened on that fateful night in the month of April. There was a power failure, the fan stopped moving. Thampuran could not bear the heat. He came out of his house and started walking up and down in the yard, with a fan in his hand. There wasn't even the faintest of breezes.

It was past midnight. It seemed certain that the power supply would not be restored that night. How could he sleep in the heat? Maddened by the heat, the Thampuran stepped out of the gate in the single dhoti that he wore and started walking down the road, fanning himself. The most dangerous walk of his life.

He felt better when a light breeze blew hesitantly across

the field in the west. The little breeze just caressed his stomach and shoulders and rushed away. Thinking that there might be airflow in the fields, the lord walked that way. His palace, which squatted huge and brooding like a hoary demon, vanished behind him.

The Thampuran's expectations were not belied. Another light breeze came rushing towards him from the fields. Like a mischievous child, the breeze got between the Thampuran's legs and tickled him. Enjoying himself, the Thampuran folded his fan and continued his westward walk. When he reached the fields, a few gusts of breeze blew in and played with the dhoti round his waist. He sat on the culvert. He had forgotten all about the heat.

The mischievous breezes hid in the fields. When he lifted his fan to fan himself, the 'breeze children' came running and giggling, clambered on his stomach and shoulders and started playing. One small imp tried to strip off his mundu. The breezes insisted on playing with the only piece of clothing he wore.

He did not feel like returning to his house. That huge house with its low ceilings and narrow windows was built by his grandfather. It was stuffy and sultry inside the house. The Thampuran could bear anything, but he could not bear the heat. The fields grew cooler as though a huge ceiling fan were rotating in the sky. The Thampuran continued to sit on the culvert. He would sit there till dawn. Then he could sleep even if the power supply had not been restored and he did not have a fan in his hand. He did not have much hope of the supply being restored that day. A grey light spread over the fields. A star fell down over the field.

The Thampuran sat and thought about things. There were a lot of things to think about. The next morning some people were coming to see Valsala, his youngest daughter. Three of his four daughters had been married off in good time. When the next day dawned, Valsala's marriage too would be fixed. The festival flag would be hoisted in the temple the next day. He was responsible for the conduct of the seven-day-long festival. The festival used to last only three days earlier. His efforts had first increased the number of days to five. From last year the celebrations had been extended to seven days. The temple festival was a celebration of the Thampuran's power and glory.

Small huts crouched like demon children on the northern side of the fields. One hut alone had a light. It looked like a drop of yellow paint in the dark. The Thampuran guessed that it must be Lakshmi's hut. What was she doing in the middle of the night with the lamp lighted, Thampuran wondered.

He could not help thinking about his own wife Parukutty. The people called her Parukutty Thampuratty. With her thin body and dark skin, she did not have his good looks. She hardly came out of the house, and was seen on rare occasions at weddings or the markets that spring up at the times of festivals. She was always conscious of the fact that she was the Thampuratty of Kallissery. If any of the local people came to visit her, she would not send him or her away empty-handed. She would give a silver rupee or some vegetables or a measure of grain as a gift. Their first three daughters looked like the Thampuran but the youngest, Valsala, looked like her mother. But the Thampuran had no fears about securing a suitable match for her in spite of that. Even if she was not very good-looking, Kunhikrishnan Thampuran's daughter would get a god-like husband. Once the people came in the morning and saw the girl this last marriage in the house would also get fixed and he would be relieved of that burden too.

There would be entertainments till the morning on all seven days of the festival. Harikatha, classical music, kathakali, dance-dramas, dance . . . The glories of the goddess of Kallissery were known even in the distant Karnataka. The maximum number of devotees came from Coorg. Accommodation for them was usually arranged in the Kallissery primary school. Boats had to be arranged for people who came from other villages . . . so many such things remained to be done. The Thampuran willingly shouldered such responsibilities. But he could not bear the heat. He prayed to the goddess to see that the power supply did not fail at least till the festival was over.

But Appu Marar who beat the drums in the temple was of a different opinion. The electricity was not something made in Kallissery. It came from some distant place, so what could the goddess do?

The wires through which the current flowed were like the rails on which the train moved. The Thampuran did not know where they came from and where they went.

The village became more visible. There was more moonlight now. The Thampuran sat on the culvert over the stream and enjoyed the night-time beauty of his land. He had not known that Kallissery could be so beautiful. He regretted the fact that he had never thought of coming out and sitting in the fields in the moonlight.

Dawn was not far away. The Thampuran got up from the culvert reluctantly. He could open the windows of the room upstairs and sleep for a while. He was very tried. His head was full of thoughts of the festival. Thoughts about his daughter's wedding also crept in now and then. It was doubtful if he would be able to sleep at all now. If he had not been Kunhikrishnan Thampuran he could have stretched out on this cool culvert and slept. Such thoughts did not usually enter his mind. He had always been proud of his noble birth. That he was a Thampuran. His only desire had always been to live up to the good name and the dignity of his noble house and then close his eyes. May god help him to do so.

He could still see light in Lakshmi's home. In the moonlight, that light spread like yellow paint that had been smeared on wet paper. The Thampuran thought that he would return home through the path on the southern side of the temple which led past her house. The impish breezes were sleeping on the breasts of the field, tired out after their mischief. The fields and their surroundings were cool as after rains.

Walking through the moonlit, narrow path, the Thampuran reached the lane that passed in front of Lakshmi's hut. Thick light spilled through the window and spread out. Was Lakshmi's husband ill? That ill-tempered and impudent fellow often complained of giddiness and shortness of breath these days.

As he climbed on to the veranda, his head knocked against the bamboo rod on which clothes had been hung out to dry. Even in that dim light he recognized the spotted blouse which Lakshmi often wore. The Thampuran knocked softly on the door. Lakshmi's face showed against the light in the window. He realized that she was sitting there sleepless. Her cheeks and the untied hair shone in the lamp light. As it was dark where he stood, Lakshmi did not recognize the Thampuran.

'Who is it?'

'Thampuran'

Lakshmi reached the door in one leap. The door moved apart with a groan. It was not unusual for the Thampuran to come to a poor man's hut and enquire about the family's wellbeing. Recently he had come to the compound and said, 'The areca palms need more water. Tell Chetty.'

How could Chetty have the time? He was fully engaged in weaving towels and selling them. The rest of the time he drank. Though he did not pay any attention to the coconut and areca palms in the compound, he looked after his Lakshmi as though she were the goddess Srilakshmi herself. After all, he had made her his own against the opposition of the whole community of weavers. After his marriage he had grown a moustache. He had done this because Lakshmi had asked him to do so. Though he had accepted his apology, the Thampuran still did not like him in his heart of hearts. He had been impudent enough to oppose the lord in the election, hadn't he? Kidnap a woman, try to defeat the Thampuran...he was an impudent fellow.

A big lamp was lighted inside. It was the light of that lamp that had drawn the Thampuran like a moth to that house. Light fell on all sides from the beautifully clean shade.

'Why haven't you put out the light and gone to sleep?'

'I am scared, Thampuran.'

'Is there no one else here? Where has Chetty gone?'

'He has gone to the town to stock up on towels.'

When the day dawned, the temple festival would start.

The towels that were sold at the Kallissery festival market were famous. The devotees who came from Coorg would buy towels even if they did not buy anything else.

'What are you scared of? There are no robbers in Kallissery.'

'I am not scared of robbers.'

'Who are you scared of then?'

'Of ghosts.'

The Thampuran felt like laughing.

'Do you stay sleepless beside this big lamp at night because you are scared of ghosts?

'I can't sleep if I am alone at night. I start seeing things if I shut my eyes,' Lakshmi was on the verge of tears.

The Thampuran felt sorry for her.

'Next time Chetty goes to the town, let me know. I'll send someone from my house to keep you company,' he consoled her. 'Put out the lamp and go to bed.'

'Don't go,' she begged. The edges of her hair seen against the light seemed to be burning.

The Thampuran was in a quandary. He knew that Chetty was not likely to return in the night. One had to take a ferry to get to Kallissery from the town. There would be no boat there at this time. The only other way was longer by four miles, over the Mekkunnu bridge. The bullock carts which took goods from Kallissery reached the town by that road. One or two bullock carts would cross over to either side every day.

'All right, I'll sit here for some time. You go to sleep.' The Thampuran prepared to sit on the veranda.

Lakshmi stopped him, 'Come in and sit.'

'Lakshmi, you are a real nuisance.'

The Thampuran bent his head so that he would not knock

against the lintel and entered the home. There was an old cot next to the wall.

'Please sit on the cot.'

He hesitated. There was no other seat in the room. It he sat on the cot, where would she sleep?

He sat reluctantly. The cot smelled of her clothes and her hair. She stood before the lamps and looked at him intently. Her honey-coloured body looked even more beautiful by the light of the lamp. Her gaze on him disturbed the Thampuran.

'Where shall I sleep now?' Her lips opened in a smile, showing small glittering teeth. Before he could say anything, she put out the light. Thampuran knew the smell of honey.

Three

The Thampuran slept next to Lakshmi as comfortably as if he were sleeping under a warm blanket while it lightly drizzles at dawn. These were rare moments of forgetfulness and release. The mind of the lord, relieved of the weights of greatness and fame, become soft and pure like the mind of a child. As the lord of the land, he had innumerable duties towards the people of Kallissery and unlimited duties to God. This consciousness had never let him live as a free man. As he saw the beautiful women of the land, the connoisseur in him would fill his mind with sensations of pleasure. Then he would realise that he was the Thampuran. Plucking his eyes away from the beauties around, he would walk away with a deep sigh.

Finally, free of all his responsibilities, the lord slept close to the honey-coloured woman. He realized what the pure joy of living was. He did not see the morning star twinkle at the edge of the sky like the stone in the woman's nose ring.

A bullock cart crossed the Mekkunnu bridge and moved towards Kallissery. The lighted lamp which hung below the cart spilled light on the rough road. The bundles of towels stacked inside moved in time with the sway of the cart. The driver waved his whip above the bullock, in a halfway stage between sleep and wakefulness.

The bell on the bullock's neck tinkled outside. The wheels of the cart groaned and became still. The lamp underneath burnt harshly with the oil exhausted.

Lakshmi woke up when she heard the sounds from the front and detached herself from the noble body of the lord. The driver of the cart unloaded the bundles of towels on the veranda. Lakshmi's husband stepped to the veranda with the sari and strings of beads he had bought for her in town. The last time he had been to the town he had bought her enough glass bangles of all colours to fill her arms. Wherever he went, he did not forget to bring gifts for his Lakshmi. After all this was the weaver women for whom he had risked his life.

'Thampuran, Thampuran…'

She shook the lord awake. He opened his eyes. His eyes showed the confusion of waking from sweet dreams to the cruel reality. 'Thampuran, you have to run…'

She stood and gathered up her hair. The lord became aware of where he was. He realized the he was in a trap. Not only his name and honour, his life too was in danger.

Heavy knocks continued to fall on the door.

'My mundu.'

'Forget about the mundu. Run away.'

She went to the back door in the dark and opened it without a sound. Pushing the lord out into the dark she pushed the bolts home again.

She lit the lamp and opened the front door. Her husband entered the house. She yawned widely and pretended to be sleepy.

'You thought I wouldn't come today, didn't you?'

'I stayed awake with the lamp lighted, till 2 o'clock,' she said sulkily and showed her displeasure.

She put the lamp on the window sill and leaned against his chest. The earrings he wore and the thick moustache rubbed against her face and neck. He gave her the sari with the golden lace and the bead-chains he had bought for her.

'This is for you to wear when you go to the temple for the festival...'

He stayed caressing her till the sun rose.

As she stood on the veranda combing her hair after her bath, Marar who played the drum at the temple came by.

'Have you heard, weaver woman? The Thampuran is missing.'

She continued with her combing, without saying anything. The hair, which had been combed with gingelly oil, gleamed like the water in the river with sunlight gilding on it.

'The Thampuran who had come out of his home to enjoy the breeze did not return home, they say.'

Lakshmi listened to all this quietly.

There was movement in the paths through the fields which spread out like the nerves of the land. Chetty was sleeping, weary after his journey. His teeth showed in a perpetual smile as he slept.

A jeep appeared some distance away. It moved forward, bucking and bouncing through the road full of holes. The clouds of dust around the jeep showed yellow in the sunlight. It was rare for a motor vehicle to be seen in Kallissery. The buses that came across the Mekkunnu bridge went straight without entering Kallissery. Two buses went that way, four times a day to Ayilakkara and Paniyar. Those who came to Kallissery had to get off the bus at the turning after the Mekkunnu bridge and walk the rest of the way. If they met a bullock cart or judka on the way they would ask for a lift.

'A jeep is coming, look,' Lakshmi pointed out.

The dust around the jeep twinkled in the sunlight like diamonds. Straightening his lungi as he got up, Chetty looked at the jeep and yawned. There were five people in the jeep. An old man with his long hair tied in front of his head sat next to the driver. One of the people in the back seat was a young woman with large gold earrings and hair parted on one side. Her lips were red with chewing betel leaves.

'I think they are going to Thampuran's house.' Lakshmi said. The only big house to the north of the fields belonged to the Thampuran. There was no other house for these important people in a jeep to go to.

'They must be the people coming to see Thampuran's daughter.'

Her guess was right. The jeep with its escort of dust clouds came to a stop before the Thampuran's house. Confusion spread in the house. Parukutty Thampuratty ran hither and thither as though her clothes had caught fire.

Valsala was not yet ready.

The sweetmeats were just getting ready in the kitchen. Everybody had been engaged in searching for the Thampuran since dawn.

The first person to get down from the jeep was Chandu Nair, with his long hair gathered into a knot in front. He held the box of chewing things in his hand. The man in the double dhoti with a thin border and a short-sleeved shirt was

Sankaran, the bridegroom to be. His ears were pierced. The Thampuran's eldest son-in-law, Uthaman Nambiar, and his nephew, Vasudevan, welcomed the guests.

'I hope the journey was all right?' Uthaman Nambiar enquired.

'It is hardly day break and it is already hot.'

'You are Sankaran's father, aren't you?'

'Yes.'

Chandu Nair moved his knot of hair to one side and wiped off the sweat. The other old man who did not wear a shirt stood with an expression of nausea on his face.

'This is?'

'My elder brother. He is travelling in a jeep for the first time. He is a little uncomfortable.'

The elder brother travelled by palanquin in his own place.

'Why don't you lie down inside for a little while?'

'No need for that. If you could get him a little water to wash his face.'

The old man, who stood there with the expression seen on the faces of pregnant women in the morning, accepted the water in the polished bronze vessel and washed his face.

The guests sat in the entrance hall of the house. Janaki took the sister of the bridegroom inside. Valsala was dressing in front of the full-length mirror. She put powder on her dark cheeks, a pottu on her forehead and darkened her eyes. The sari would not get tied properly however many times she took it off and wore it again. Either too much of it would be tucked in and the sari would rise above her ankles. Or there would be too many pleats. Finally she managed somehow with the help of Vasudevan's wife, Karthyayini. Valsala had worn a sari only once before. That was for the temple festival at Kallissery.

'No boy from my family has ever gone to see a girl before. The right thing is for the elders and sisters to go and see the girl. But my son very stubbornly insisted that he was coming.'

Uthaman Nambiar laughed. The young man with his hair slicked back with oil sat shyly, head bent. The buttons on his shirt were of gold.

'Your name?'

'Sankaran.'

'He is my last boy. The next three are girls.'

Chandu Nair had nine children. When he was about to open the box of chewing things, Nambiar stopped him, 'After a drop of tea…'

Valsala appeared at the top of the dark staircase. Her steps sounded on the old wooden stairs as she walked down, accompanied by Karthyayini. The gaze of Sankaran's sister, Nani, fell first on the ornaments she wore. Nani guessed that the necklace of coins would be at least five sovereigns. In her estimate the bangles worn up to the elbows and the chains and necklaces would weigh at least forty sovereigns. She was an expert at assessing the weight of gold worn at one glance.

'Sankaran, come inside,' Nani called.

Chandu Nair, his elder brother and the others entered the inner room and sat around the table. Appam, ada and other eatables were served on small plates on the table laden with dust. Chandu Nair's elder brother could feel nausea coming on once more. Sankaran's heart beat like a clock when Valsala came in with the tea.

Suddenly something occurred to Chandu Nair. 'Isn't Kunhikrishnan Thampuran home?'

The old man's voice contained surprise. And irritation. They had come after informing the family of the programme. Even the exact time of arrival had been conveyed. Common courtesy demanded that the Thampuran come to receive them when the jeep arrived at the gate. And he had not deigned to come out and meet them even after so long…

Uthaman Nambiar went pale at the question. Parukutty Thampuratty felt faint.

'He's gone to the ferry dock. To look for you.'

'But we had informed him that we were coming by jeep.'

The Thampuran's son-in-law had no answer to that.

Something else occurred to Chandu Nair. He remembered that he had seen the judka in the shed and the horse outside, as he got out of the jeep. There was something wrong.

'Serve Sankaran with the sweet, child,' Thampuratty said.

Valsala obeyed. Sankaran's face changed colour from shyness. Thampuratty herself served the old man and his brother. But Chandu Nair sat with a black face. Though dark, the girl was all right. It was the Thampuran's absence that irritated him. He believed that he was as important in his place as Kunhikrishnan Thampuran was in Kallissery.

'Please don't get up without eating anything.'

'Let Thampuran come.'

When he saw the old man get up, the elder brother also got up. And so did the others. Only Sankaran remained sitting. When he looked at Valsala who stood near the door with her face half turned away, moonlight filled his mind.

His father cleared his throat rather loudly. Understanding the import of that, Sankaran got up reluctantly and went to the veranda.

'We are going...'

'Please don't. We have sent a man to the ferry dock. Father will reach here any minute...'

'Nambiar, I also come from a good family. Tell me the truth whatever it is. If Thampuran has gone to the ferry dock why is it that the horse and judka are here?'

Uthaman Nambiar once again had no answer. Parukutty Thampuratty's heart melted. Her eyes filled with tears.

'Valsala's father went to stand on the road last night because of the heat. He has not come back. Only god knows where he has gone...'

The old man laughed out a loud. 'My dear Parukuttyamma, need you try these tricks on me? Ettan, Nani, Sankaran, let us go...'

Nani tucked in the pallu of her sari at her waist, picked up her umbrella and stepped out of the house in a hurry. The others followed. Sankaran got out reluctantly. He looked back twice. His heart turned at the sight of Valsala who went running inside, wiping her eyes.

'Father, I liked the girl...'

'Who is bothered about your likes?' The old man shouted.

He combed the long hair which had fallen loose into a tighter knot. The jeep moved, spreading dust and mud. Thampuratty sobbed. Uthaman Nambiar sat with his head in his hands.

The quarry had formed when they had taken stones to build a school in Kallissery. The water that had collected in it had now dried up in the heat of the sun. Plants and creepers had grown thickly at the edges of the big hole. When the jeep reached near the school, Thampuran, who had been hiding in the quarry, slowly lifted his head. He had very good eyesight and had no problem in recognizing Chandu Nair. He wished to run out and stop the jeep. But how could he come out of the quarry with no clothes?

When the jeep passed the school and went out of sight, he pulled in his head like a tortoise and hid again.

Four

By midday, the quarry and its surroundings were deserted. The theyyams did not dance during the day on the first day of the festival. Few people went to the temple because of that. When he saw nobody on the path, the Thampuran became hopeful. He parted the overgrown creepers and stood on his toes to peer outside. There was not a soul within sight. The whole place was in the grip of a heat-induced lassitude.

Calling upon the gods to protect him, Thampuran slowly pulled himself out of the quarry. The mimosa shut their eyes in shyness when he came near them. His legs ached. And burnt from the scratches from plants. Once out of the quarry, he hid behind the tree at the side. He squatted behind the trunk and looked around. Nothing living moved anywhere. The only sound was the tired cawing of crows in the heat.

Folding his hands and praying once more, Thampuran came out from behind the tree and took a couple of steps forward. The pale, yellow sunlight fell on his body and shocked him. The Thampuran of Kallissery was standing without a stitch of clothing on the public road in the middle of the day. The shock of the sunlight weakened him. His legs felt as though they had become paralysed. He got back down into the quarry with its touch-me-nots and scratchy bushes and hid himself among them.

He realized that he would not be able to step out during the day and reach his home. How could a noble lord walk through his own village naked as on the day he was born? It would be better to die. Kunhikrishnan Thampuran valued his good name more than his life. He had taught the people of Kallissery that they had to preserve their self-respect even at the cost of their heads. He had never lent his support to anything which involved loss of face.

The river that flowed to the west looked like molten lava. The sun burnt itself out. In a little while Kallissery would grow dark. All movement would stop.

The helpless Thampuran crouched in the quarry like a bird that had lost its wings. How could he go home without any clothes? His whole body was burning from the bites of insects. His mind was also burning. This was the second night he was spending in the quarry.

He was exhausted and could not hide any longer without food and sleep. He had to get out of this hole this night, no matter what methods he had to use. God had to show him a way. The Thampuran's hands folded and eyes raised themselves to the sky. A feeble rocket rose from outside the temple like the cry of a helpless man in search of divine help, and vanished in the sky.

He waited for the shadows to deepen. He could not escape out of this watery grave without the help of darkness.

When he thought of how he had spent the day, he felt faint. Hot and sweaty. Hungry and thirsty. And above all, afraid of disgrace. He was on the verge of unconsciousness.

The darkness deepened. The Thampuran's only hope was the dark. He had lost the light.

A brightness spread afar among the dark coconut palms. The light came from the temple. The lights dimmed his hopes. Light now frightened him.

He now hoped that the power would fail and Kallissery would be immersed in darkness. In darkness lay his refuge.

Everything started with electricity. It was because the power had failed and the fan had stopped rotating that he had got out of the house and got entangled in the spell cast by the weaver woman.

The light fell on the pillars that had been installed at intervals on either side of the path. The light fell right up to the edge of the quarry. The Thampuran shrank back as though he were a thief on whom the light of a torch had fallen.

Whom could he blame? Ayilakkara and Paniyar still did not have electricity. The Mekkunnu bridge was lighted only by two kerosene lamps which spluttered dimly at either end. The people knew that electricity had reached Kallissery before it reached anywhere else only due to the efforts of its Thampuran.

The Thampuran cursed the electricity. His opinion that all newfangled things caused harm to human beings was reaffirmed. Who had thought that the effort he had made for the good of his place would result in problems for himself?

The Thampuran also felt angry with Raman Chetty. Why had he returned at that odd time from the town? Could he not have stayed over at the town that night? Hadn't he come in a bullock cart in the middle of the night just to put the Thampuran in a hole?

As it is, Chetty was an insubordinate sort of fellow, an impudent fellow, who had opposed him in the election with the help of jealous and treacherous outsiders, then had fallen at his feet and begged pardon. The Thampuran could have chased him away from Kallissery forever. He was surprised at the way all his good deeds turned out to be harmful for himself. He decided that he would have to reassess his inherited notions on the results of deeds and of virtue and sin. But first he had to get out of the quarry.

The fireworks boomed near the river. Birds rose startled from the fruit tree that stood on the slope of the quarry and then returned to their nests. The Thampuran realized that it was time for the ceremonial bath of the goddess. The goddess would bathe in the Kallissery river and go to the temple with the accompaniment of music and drums. The festive mood would heighten with this ceremony.

Usually it was the Thampuran who decorated the statue of the goddess with sandalwood paste and her special jewels. It was his right to bow first before the goddess who stood smiling, decorated with sandalwood paste and clad in rich garments. After him, Parukutty Thampuratty and the rest of his family would render obeisance. This custom had never been broken before. Why had the goddess who had showered blessings on him for so long deserted him? Was the sin he had committed bad enough to deserve the kind of torture he was going through now? Other lords slept around. But he had never touched a woman other than his Parukutty Thampuratty. He had forbidden love marriages among the people of Kallissery for their own good. The last love marriage in the place had been that of Raman Chetty and the weaver woman. The Thampuran sat like a statue, his chin on his hand.

Drumbeats rose from the banks of the river. The goddess would start towards the temple now. Kunhanpoosari used to be the Vellattu oracle before. Though he had lost his eyesight he continued to act as the oracle in the temple for some time, but now it was Kurumban from Ayilakkara who wore the red silk and carried the sword before the goddess. The light which glimmered through the trees grew brighter.

The bathing procession of the goddess reached the road on its way to the temple. Lamps filled with ghee were lighted in front of all the houses. The Thampuran crouched lower when the light fell into the quarry. He should have been in the front of the procession with the goddess, clad in gold-bordered clothes. Instead he ducked his head into the undergrowth like a wild animal who had seen his predator. Shadows and light played over him and moved away.

When the procession passed, he came alive again. Lifting his head from the bushes, he thought about his sad situation once more. If he was not able to get out of this hell hole this night he would have to stay there till the end of the festival. From the next day the festivities would go on round the clock. The theyyams would dance and people would be moving up and down the street.

Kallissery would not sleep till the end of the festival now.

He sat on a stone, picking out the lice that had attached themselves to his body. A bee troubled him on and off; he had seen a beehive on the tree on the western side of the quarry. What would he do if the hive was disturbed and the bees attacked him in a group? Where could he run? May god prevent such a cruel fate!

He sat on the stone, faint with hunger and thirst, and thought of ways to escape from this bind. There was a blind man in Kallissery. That was Kunhanpoosari. The Thampuran's only hope was that man. If he walked this way just once, the Thampuran could escape. He was the only man in front of whom the Thampuran could stand without embarrassment in this state. Being blind, he would not see the state Thampuran was in. If he could get the towel that the poosary usually slung over his shoulder, it would be sufficient. He could cover his nakedness and walk through the night to his house. Maybe it would not really reach his knees. But it was certainly better than walking around without any clothes.

Each time a shadow climbed on to the road from the lane or the fields, the Thampuran would lift his head and look expectantly. Once it was his nephew Vasudevan. He thought of calling out and asking him to throw a dhoti to the quarry. But he got rid of the idea immediately. His nephew was so terrified of him that he was likely to piss in his clothes if his uncle called his name a little loudly. To stand before such a nephew without clothes was impossible. He hid behind the tree till Vasudevan vanished from sight. People came and went. Only Kunhanpoosari did not appear. Would a blind man come alone across that road to watch the festival? What logic was there in expecting that? The weary lord had lost his power of reasoning as well.

When the star that betokened midnight rose, the Thampuran got ready for a risky venture. Though the drums still beat feebly from the distant temple, the movement of people had decreased. Once in a while, a Kallissery man would walk by like a wanderer who had lost his way. Dawn was not far off. The Thampuran lifted his head and looked around. A torch glimmered and dimmed some way beyond in the areca-nut grove.

The Thampuran did not have the courage to walk through the public road with its electric lamps. He had to go across other people's compounds and take short-cuts chanting the names of gods mentally and calling on his ancestors to protect him. The Thampuran stood up slowly. He looked around once more to make sure that there was no one around and climbed up out of the quarry. The Thampuran's body shone in the moonlight once he was out of the hole. He circled the quarry and got down into the dried-up stream to the north of it. A dog howled somewhere nearby. The house just beyond the stream belonged to Choyi Kuruppu who taught at the local school. The house had no light. The Thampuran crawled across the low wall and into the compound. The dried-up mud-plaster broke into bits and fell into the waterway. The Thampuran hid behind the tamarind tree as soon as he got into the compound. He had to cross the schoolmaster's broad compound under cover of shadows and get down into the lane behind Appu Menon master's house. With that he would have successfully completed the first stage of his dangerous journey.

When he had moved a few steps, he saw torches glimmer in the west. He stood still behind the tree and listened carefully. If the people from the temple went across to the road he had nothing to be afraid of.

But when they turned away from the road and towards the north, his limbs felt weak. That big group with lots of men, women and children carried a number of torches. They had to be people from Pandiyar. One could reach Pandiyar easily by crossing the dried-up stream and walking northwards through the fields. The light of the torches came closer. The children and women were chattering and giggling.

If he went back a few steps and stood behind the old tamarind tree it was probable that no one would see him. But he knew that if the school master woke up because of the lights and sound and turned on the light in the veranda he would not be able to escape. His eyes filled with darkness at the thought of it. Oh god…why these trials…

The Thampuran crawled back into the stream. He lost his grip and that big, naked body rolled into the dry bed of the stream. He somehow stumbled onto his feet and rushed towards the quarry. He fell on the road in that mad rush. A dog barked loudly somewhere nearby. The Thampuran lay inert at the bottom of the quarry and let out a long sigh.

The light of the torches twinkled above the quarry. The children and men moved away noisily. A stray dog come to the side of the dry stream and barked loud and long…

The people from Pandiyar crossed the stream and continued their walk through the lanes. The glimmer of the torches moved away across the grey fields.

Soon the sky paled. A cool wind started blowing. The people of Kallissery returned from the festival with eyes drooping with sleep.

Five

Thampuran's house, which had always been as active as an anthill, now resembled a house of death. It was four days since Parukutty Thampuratty had eaten anything. Though the front yard was crowded with servants and dependants, no one spoke. Local people kept coming and going.

'Let us also go there,' Raman Chetty suggested.

'You go, I am not coming.'

'After all, he's our Thampuran.'

Lakshmi did not say anything. Chetty had no ill feeling towards the Thampuran. Though he was old fashioned and stubborn, he had always been full of affection for the village and the villagers. The whole place was upset by his startling disappearance. It would be only polite to go and enquire about it.

Chetty took out his blue shirt and wore it. He did not have much time to stand around and talk. Business was very good in the festival market. He had sold about three hundred towels the previous day. It had been a wise decision to stop milling oil and start selling towels. The number of devotees from Coorg had increased this year. Each of them bought three-four towels.

'Wait a minute. I'm also coming.' Lakshmi changed her mind. She had managed to sink the Thampuran's dhoti in the Kallissery river quietly.

'You need a little more powder on your cheeks.'

'Where do you think I am going? To celebrate a wedding?'

Every day was a celebration for him when he was with her. Both of them started walking towards the Thampuran's house. Chetty's golden earring glinted in the midday sun.

The village was a place of gloom in spite of the festival. The drums from the temple sounded like a dirge.

'Children disappear. Now it has reached such a stage that grown-ups have started disappearing.' That was the schoolmaster returning from the Thampuran's house. His school was closed to provide shelter to the pilgrims who had come for the festival.

'Is there no clue, master?'

'Hey Chetty, you are an ass. What clue could there be? Thampuran is not alive. That's all.' The schoolmaster walked on.

'He must have fallen into the river in the dark and been dragged away when he went out for a walk in the night,' Chetty spoke as though to himself.

Parukutty Thampuratty lay still on the cot with its smell of antiquity. Her normally dark face was darker with tears that had dried.

'Mother, have a little gruel. How long can you lie like this?' Janaki came and stood beside her.

'Let your father come,'

'Of course, he will come. Where will he go? You have something now.' She moved the dish of hot gruel closer to her mother.

'I am going mad with worry,' Thampuratty wiped her eyes.

'If you lie like this, without food and drink, you'll fall ill soon.'

'I don't care. Why should I live now…?'

'But we don't know what has happened to father. Let us wait till we have some definite news.'

People had gone in all directions in search of the Thampuran. Uthaman Nambiar had gone to the town to make a written complaint to the police. The Thampuran had earlier ordered that no policeman should be seen in Kallissery. He was enough to keep law and order in his land. Finally, the police had to come to Kallissery on account of the Thampuran. They enjoyed the joke. Asking questions as they pleased in the Thampuran's absence, they strolled through Kallissery.

Kunhikrishnan Thampuran's relatives were scattered far and near. Hearing the news, they got into boats and palanquins and reached Kallissery. Some of them used the opportunity to go into the temple and watch the festival celebrations, and to buy the famous Kallissery towels. Raman Chetty's purse grew fatter and fatter.

The festival was nearly over. Kallissery was full of pilgrims on the last day. The Coorgis were bathing and resting in the school building.

Valsala had not gone to the festival so far. She had kept aside money to go to the market and buy bangles and ribbons and clips. She had such dreams… She had liked Sankaran who came to see her though he seemed very shy. She had been hurt badly when Chandu Nair gathered everybody together and returned immediately in the jeep. She had thought she would go to the festival to forget everything. But how could she go to the festival when the house had turned into a house of death? With whom could she go?

'You are not fated to enjoy anything.' She told herself as she sat before the full-length mirror. The mirror was filled with her dark face.

She too did not understand what had happened to her father. He was so systematic in everything. He would never go out without telling mother when he was going. She had seen her father stroll on the road with a fan in his hand as she sat by the window reading a novel that night. She had put out the kerosene lamp and gone to bed when she felt sleepy. When she woke up in the morning, her father was not there.

'Valsala, do you know where your father is?'

'I did not see him.'

She felt like laughing when she saw how worried her mother was the next morning. Was father a small child to be fussed over like this?

The Thampuran would sometimes go to the stables to pet his horse. He was very fond of that horse which had something of his own majesty. He would not permit the driver to beat it unnecessarily.

But he was not in the stables either that day, 'Oh god, where do I look for him now?'

'Thampuratty, don't stand on the road. You go back. I'll go look for Thampuran,' Ambu had said.

The water that had been heated for the Thampuran's bath cooled. The warm milk and gruel grew cold. Thampuran did not come. Thampuratty sat waiting with her eyes fixed outside.

It was now the seventh day. Thampuratty's ninety-year-old father came and got down from the palanquin.

'What do I have to live for now, father...?' Parukutty Thampuratty wept.

Her father called Ambu to himself and questioned him secretly. All the lords had some illicit relationship or the other. Did Kunhikrishnan Thampuran also have some such connection in the neighbourhood of Kallissery? Ambu's face reddened when he heard this. He forgave the man only because he was Thampuratty's father. The Thampuran had never even lifted his head to look at another woman. Look at the way the old man's crooked mind worked...

'Then where do you think he has gone?'

'Only the man up there knows,' Ambu pointed to the sky.

Uthaman Nambiar and Vasudevan sat on the veranda. Both of them were silent. Had they given up hope? There was no place left to look now. The ferryman swore that the Thampuran had not crossed the river. The bus people who crossed the Mekkunnu bridge were equally sure that the Thampuran had not gone to Pandiyar and Ayilakkara either.

He had not crossed the river. He had not crossed the bridge. Nor had he crossed the fields. Thampuran's disappearance was a riddle to which there was no answer.

The search and the questioning had just about ended. The family sat around in the house silently.

The Thampuran will never come back. He is dead.

They had all started believing that. The festival also suffered in the Thampuran's absence. The Harikatha people from Madurai did not land up. The people from Virajpetta had a fight with the Kallissery people. There was loss in the festival market. If Thampuran had been there, none of this would have happened.

'The place is going to the dogs. You wait and see,' the blind Kunhanpoosari predicted. The stars were against Kallissery.

When the sun had climbed into the sky, the schoolmaster came panting up with the day's newspaper. It was usually noon by the time the morning paper reached Kallissery. Thampuran had insisted that everyone who knew reading and writing in Kallissery should read the newspaper everyday. In spite of that, only six newspapers were sold in Kallissery.

'What is it, master?' Uttaman Nambiar asked anxiously. Everyone was always afraid. They were all waiting for some calamity.

The schoolmaster who had run all the way stood in the yard panting. Even if the house had caught fire he ought not to have run at his age. He had reached pensionable age four years back. But knowing the family's state of poverty, the Thampuran had got his term extended. He was troubled by asthma as well as by age.

'Why don't you say something?'

'Thampuran's gone...'

Loud cries started from inside. Uttaman Nambiar took the paper from the schoolmaster. Though it was that morning's newspaper, you would have thought it was at least a decade old from the colour of the paper.

'What does it say in the paper?' Thampuratty's father moved closer. Uttaman Nambiar swallowed. Vasudavan felt faint.

'Why is everyone silent? What does the paper say?' Thampuratty's father was getting upset. The school master sat with his head in his hands. His panting was becoming an asthmatic wheeze.

'They haven't identified the person. How can they? It is seven days!'

Bloated with river water, the face eaten by fish...

The people who had been going to the festival broke off in groups. How could the people of Kallissery celebrate any festival now? A section of the crowd suggested that the fireworks display be abandoned as a sign of respect to their Thampuran.

'Don't make a row,' Uttaman Nambiar went in and told the women. 'It is not certain at all that it is father. Let us go and find out for sure.'

But the women did not stop crying. No one was willing to believe him.

The electric light was on inside though it was daytime. Uttaman Nambiar's eyes fell on the big framed photograph on the wall. The Thampuran with a gold medal on his broad chest and a proud smile on his face. The district collector from the town had pinned that medal on him.

Uttaman Nambiar bent his head and came out. He started out towards Alathur where the dead body had been thrown ashore. It was sixteen miles away. Would the body be there when he reached? The coachman brought the horse out of the stables and tied it to the judka. Two of the local people also set out with Nambiar. They would go by judka up to the Mekkunnu bridge, from there to the town by bus and then hire a jeep to take them to Alathur.

Vasudevan, who had lost all courage, joined the women inside and wept. He was a nervous type anyway. Parukutty Thampuratty fainted and fell. Valasala's eyes were red with continuous weeping.

The crowd in the front yard increased and soon overflowed onto the road. Seeing a crowd, some of the hawkers brought their wares and tried to sell balloons and sweets there. The Thampuran's house and its surroundings became the festival field.

Then far off in the deserted road, a wild-looking man appeared. His body was covered with dust. His hair and beard were full of lice. He had covered his nakedness with a few broad leaves strung on a wild creeper. He walked towards the crowd like a primitive tribal who had lost his way from the forest...

The Thampuran's house and surroundings suddenly grew silent.

Thampuran...someone said from the crowd. The people were stunned as though the sky had fallen down.

The Thampuran stepped into the yard tentatively like a child learning to walk. He did not show any hurry to go in and cover his nakedness with clothes.

He walked to the well through the people who stood as though stunned and drew up a bucketful of water and drank it. It was the first time in his life that he was drawing a bucket of water for himself. After he had quenched his thirst with the clear water he turned around. Family, relatives, dependants, local people...he looked at all of them and smiled the innocent smile of a child.

About the Author

M. Mukundan is one of the most reputed fiction writers in Kerala today. Author of over forty books comprising novels, collections of short stories, a play and a study of modernity, he made his literary debut in the 1960s publishing stories. His bestselling books include *On the Banks of the Mayyazhi*, *Delhi Gathakal* and *The Bells Are Ringing in Haridwar*. Some of his novels are taught in universities in Kerala. He has won many awards and honours, including the Sahitya Akademi award; Ezhuthachan Puraskaram, the highest literary award conferred by the Government of Kerala; Chevalier of the Arts and Letters, conferred by the Government of France; and the First Crossword award for Indian language fiction in English translation.

Four of his novels were adapted into feature films, with *God's Mischief* winning the Kerala State Film Award for best film. He also won the Kerala State Film Award for the best screenplay and Kerala Film Critics' Award for the best feature film story. His novel, *Kesavan's Lamentation*, rendered in English by A.J. Thomas, also won the Crossword Book Award in 2006.

He served as president of the Kerala Sahitya Akademi from 2006 to 2010. His stories and novels have been translated into English and French and published in the USA and France. He lives in Mahe, his hometown in Kerala.

About the Author

About the Translator

Prema Jayakumar was born in Kerala and studied in Kochi and Bangalore. She does translations from Malayalam into English and writes for periodicals. Her translated works include Mukundan's *God's Mischief* (*Daivathinte Vikrithikal*) among many others by well-known Malayalam authors.

Her works have been published by Penguin and the Sahitya Akademi. She has retold the Ramayana, the Mahabharata and other stories from the Puranas for Mango Books and Real Reads (UK). Married, with one son, she stays mostly in Kochi but loves to travel.

The HarperCollins–Ratna Sagar Translation Series

Ratna Sagar is an Indian publishing company founded in 1982; Ratna Books, its translations-only imprint, was launched in 2017. The aim of the Ratna Sagar translation list has been to bring acclaimed works written in the Indian languages to a wider readership in English translation, and the focus has been to ensure the quality of the translations, to provide the reader with a seamless reading experience.

Forty-two books have been published in the Ratna Sagar translation list so far, all in hardback. The books have been received well by readers and have met with critical acclaim from the media; many of the books have also won or been nominated for literary awards.

HarperCollins is proud to partner with Ratna Sagar to bring this list of high-quality translations to readers in paperback editions, publishing under HarperCollins's prestigious Perennial imprint.

READ MORE

Havan by Mallikarjun Hiremath

Leaf, Water and Flow by Avadhoot Dongare

Parthiban's Dream by Kalki Krishnamurthy

Prison Notes of a Woman Activist by Bellapu Anuradha

The Bells Are Ringing in Haridwar by M. Mukundan

Dukhi Dadiba by Dadi Edulji Taraporewala

After Yesterday and Other Stories by Appaduari Muttulingam

The Sixth Finger by Malayatoor Ramakrishnan

A Faceless Evening and Other Stories by Gangadhar Gadgil

If a River and Other Stories by Kula Saikia

On a River's Bank by A. Madhavan

Echoes of the Veena and Other Stories by R. Chudamani

Here I Am and Other Stories by P. Sathyavathi

The Rock That Was Not and Other Stories by Githanjali

The Story of Being Useless and Three Contexts of a Writer by Avadhoot Dongare

Mirror in the Hall and Other Stories by Prakash Bal Joshi

The Songs of Life and Other Stories by Vijaya Rajadhyaksha

Jalasamadhi and Other Stories by A. Sethumadhavan

Kadambari – The Flower Girl by A. Sethumadhavan

The Scent of Happiness by R. Vatsala

Asprishya Ganga and Other Stories by Kolakaluri Enoch

Alka and Other Stories by Goutam Das

If there is a God and Other Stories by Imayam

Ananta Jeevanam by Kolakaluri Enoch

The Stepmother and Other Stories by Laxmibai Abhyankar

Cracked Glass Jar and Other Stories by Chandra Latha

A Fine Thread and Other Stories by B. Jeyamohan

Forever Yours, Krishna by Indira Parthasarathy

Mayaloka by Poornachandra Tejaswi

The Go-Between and Other Stories by Ghanshyam Desai

The Masked Face and Two Other Stories by Vaasanthi

Vasudeva ... The Wanderer Prince by Sanghadasagani Vacaka

Randhi: Of Power and Desire by Kolakaluri Enoch

HarperCollins *Publishers* India

At HarperCollins India, we believe in telling the best stories and finding the widest readership for our books in every format possible. We started publishing in 1992; a great deal has changed since then, but what has remained constant is the passion with which our authors write their books, the love with which readers receive them, and the sheer joy and excitement that we as publishers feel in being a part of the publishing process.

Over the years, we've had the pleasure of publishing some of the finest writing from the subcontinent and around the world, including several award-winning titles and some of the biggest bestsellers in India's publishing history. But nothing has meant more to us than the fact that millions of people have read the books we published, and that somewhere, a book of ours might have made a difference.

As we look to the future, we go back to that one word—a word which has been a driving force for us all these years.

Read.